The Rathcael Codex

A James Tolliver San Francisco Mystery

By Greg Fowlkes

Includes a special preview of

The Blood Red Sands of Mars Part One from the Murder on Mars Series

THE RATHCAEL CODEX

Published by The Fictional Press

The Fictional Press, an imprint of Intrepid Ink, LLC, provides full publishing services to authors of fiction and non-fiction books, eBooks and websites. From editing to formatting, to publishing, to marketing, Intrepid Ink gets your creative works into the hands of the people who want to read them.

Find out more at www.thefictionalpress.com.

ISBN 13: 978-1-943403-51-6

Printed in the United States of America

CHAPTER 1

The phone call came as I was staring out the office window. A late afternoon thunderstorm had just ended, bringing with it the promise of an end to a winter that had been cold and damp in a way that you only get in San Francisco. I could still see flashes of lightning illuminating clouds in the distance. Below in the pools of water on the pavement I could see the oily reflection of the neon sign above the window of the diner across the street. Another sign flashed with the promise of "Cocktails" announcing the bar next door. I would have been tempted to open the window for a breath of fresh air, but the window was stuck shut with layers of paint.

I turned from the window to pick the telephone receiver off the instrument on the desk. Except for a bottle of rye with a few remaining fingers of amber liquid and the empty tumbler the desk was bare. Business had been slow lately. Maybe the weather had been too foggy for husbands to go out and cheat on their wives or for wives to cheat on their husbands, it was either that or the spouses had ceased to care. It had been that kind of a winter. It had even been too depressing for there to be much in the way of insurance fraud and skip tracing, the backbones of this business.

I brought the receiver to my mouth and said, "James Tolliver Detective Agency. How can I help you?"

"Is this Mr. Tolliver speaking?" a voice squeaked from the phone. The high pitch was due to more than the tinny qualities of the instrument. It was a voice one could instantly take a dislike to.

"This is James Tolliver," I answered in the polite voice I reserved for potential clients.

"Mr. Tolliver, my name is Edward Fenchurch. I am the business agent of Mr. Timaeus Brockington. Would you be available for an urgent commission?"

Given the current state of my bank balance I was ready for any kind of commission that paid, whether it was urgent or not.

"I believe I have some time available in my schedule," I answered trying not to sound too eager.

"Mr. Brockington would want your full attention until the completion of this matter."

"That can be arranged," I replied. "For a price."

"That should not pose a problem, Mr. Tolliver."

"Exactly what is the nature of this—commission?" I asked.

"Mr. Brockington wishes you to find something of his."

"Finding things is a specialty of mine. Exactly what am I looking for?"

Usually at this point I discover the what that is missing is a wife or wayward daughter.

"I think that Mr. Brockington would rather inform you of that himself. Could you come out to the house at say seven o'clock this evening?"

That would interrupt my dinner hour, but then, the diner across the street was open all night. "I think I can manage that, Mr. Fenchurch. Can you give me the address?"

He gave me an address just to the west of Nob Hill that made me thing that I should raise my daily rates.

"And Mr. Tolliver—," he said.

"Yes?"

"This matter must be handled discretely. Please don't mention it to anyone."

"Don't worry. I'm always discrete." There are others that would beg to differ on that, but I know when to keep my trap shut. "I'll be there at seven."

CHAPTER 2

After a quick sandwich in the diner across the street I flagged down a cab outside and gave the driver the address Fenchurch had given me. Between dinner and the cab fare, I was down to my last few bucks. If I didn't get an advance, I'd probably end up having to hoof it back home.   It wouldn't be the first time. Unfortunately, being a private investigator doesn't come with a regular paycheck.

From what I knew of Brockington from the papers, his family had made a fortune selling supplies to miners during the era of the Comstock Lode. They had made a second fortune during the rebuilding of the city after the 1906 quake, and the current head of the family had used that stake to make a third fortune supplying meat to the military during the war. The resulting fortune had been invested conservatively, and as a result had weathered the depression more or less intact.

The cab dropped me off in front of the house. I say house, but it was really more of a mansion, one of those Italianate piles that had been built using the silver that had been dug out of Nevada in the later part of the eighteen hundreds. Unlike some of its neighbors to the east of Nob Hill, it had survived the earthquake and the ensuing fire without significant damage. I paid off the cabby and told him not to wait.

The house was grand enough, three stories of gray stone, but it was starting to show its age. There was an air of genteel neglect about the shrubbery along the street, and the paint on the window frames could have used some attention, but it still presented an imposing façade to the street. A set of steps led up to large double doors about ten feet tall placed symmetrically in the center. I assumed that that was the main entrance. I also assumed that it was the entrance I was supposed to use and not the tradesman's entrance which would have been someplace to the rear.

I was about to knock on the door, not having spotted a bell push, when one of the panels swung open. Behind the door was a tall, cadaverous looking gentleman in a black tail coat. I made another assumption that this was the butler and not Brockington. It seemed a safe bet.

"Mr. Tolliver?" the butler said. It was framed as a question, but the tone indicated it as fact.

"Yes," I replied. I sensed that any witty repartee would be wasted.

"If you will follow me, Mr. Brockington has asked that you wait in the study. He will join you momentarily."

I followed Jeeves through the entry hall and a pair of doors only slightly less impressive than those out front. The "study" proved to be a room about thirty by forty feet. A massive fireplace with an equally large fire going in it took up one end. Shelves of leather bound books lined the walls. Various "curios" were spaced around the room. Everything else was dark wood and gloom. A pair of chandeliers twelve feet overhead and a number of sconces along the walls tried to lighten the atmosphere without much effect.

A minute or so after the butler had withdrawn, a slight man about five eight and a hundred thirty pounds entered the room. His thinning blonde hair was slicked back and he had black rimmed glasses with round lenses. He was dressed in a dark, pin-striped suit that fit him perfectly, complemented by the perfectly folded silk pocket square peeking out of his breast pocket. His shoes were black and polished.

"Mr. Tolliver? Edward Fenchurch." As I knew who I was, I assumed this was the man on the phone. The voices matched. He held out a hand which I took. While not exactly limp, the handshake wasn't what you'd call "firm" either.

"Mr. Brockington will join us in a moment. He will explain everything then."

"That's fine," I said, "I'm in no hurry. Nice place Mr. Brockington has here."

"Yes," Fenchurch replied either ignoring or not recognizing the sarcasm in my tone. "Mr. Brockington has some very fine pieces. He's quite a collector of antiquities, especially books. Of course, the best items are in the library."

That didn't surprise me. After all, the "study," only had a few thousand books on the shelves. Of course, most of the collection would be in the library.

Fenchurch proved not to be much of a conversationalist. I spent a few minutes cooling my heels staring at the spines of books. Finally, the set of doors at the other end of the study opened to reveal the owner of the house.

Timeus Brockington was tall, in his late fifties, with dark hair brushed back against the sides of his head. He used crutches to get around. While his shoulders and forearms would have been a credit to a blacksmith, I could see that under the tailored pants his legs were wasted, the results, I later discovered of a riding accident that had left him paralyzed from the waist down. A Negro attendant in a white jacket hovered discretely in the background.

Following in Brockington's wake was a nice looking dame. Nice looking that is, if one had fantasies about schoolmarms or high school librarians. Her brunette hair was pulled back into a bun and her curves were restrained by a severe dark suit that did nothing to conceal a pair of shapely calves that ended in sensible shoes. A pair of horn rimmed tortoise shell glasses completed the package.

Brockington laboriously took a seat behind the eight foot long library table that occupied one end of the study. Once seated, he motioned to a chair across from him and said, "Have a seat, Mr. Tolliver." Fenchurch and the dame remained standing.

I sat in the chair. It was hard and uncomfortable.

"I believe in getting down to business, Mr. Tolliver. Something of mine has been stolen. I want it back. I am prepared to pay a reasonable amount for its return. Are you prepared, Mr. Tolliver, to devote all your energies to this task until it is completed? I will pay your usual rates and expenses with a substantial bonus when the item is restored to me?"

"How substantial?" I asked.

"Five thousand dollars, Mr. Tolliver."

"That's certainly substantial, Mr. Brockington. Just exactly what is the nature of the item you wish returned."

"A book, Mr. Tolliver."

"It's none of my business, Mr. Brockington, but judging from this room, it would seem that you have plenty of reading material."

"You jest, Mr. Tolliver. I like that in a man. So few people do that with me."

"That's me. Always ready with the quip. Just what is so special about this book that it's worth five grand?

"Oh, far more than five grand, as you say. The book is unique. It is, in fact, an eleventh century manuscript produced by an Irish monk. There is not another like it in the world. For a number of years it had disappeared from sight and was feared lost. Recently it resurfaced, and I bought it at auction through an agent, a local dealer in used books. For reasons of my own, I preferred that my association with the purchase not become public knowledge. The book was supposed to be delivered to this dealer yesterday. He was then to pass it on to me. Last night the dealer was murdered and the book was taken. I wish you to recover it. It is as simple as that."

"It must be some book. What are the police saying about it?"

"The police seem more concerned about the death of the dealer than the book."

"They can be unreasonable that way," I commented. "They also tend to take a dim view of private dicks butting into murder investigations. Not that that will stop me, but it will complicate things."

"That will not be a problem, Mr. Tolliver. As you can imagine, I know some rather highly placed people, people who owe me or would like to owe me favors. The police commissioner has promised me the full cooperation of the department. That includes access to the crime scene and any reports of the investigation."

"That should make things easier," I said. Not that I believed it. Forced cooperation and willing cooperation were two completely different things. I couldn't see the bulls welcoming an outsider crashing their party.

"Who's the detective in charge?"

"I was told Miller, Detective Lt. Miller. Do you know him?"

"Yeah. We're not buddies, but as far as I know I'm not on his bad side. That should be okay."

"If not, contact Fenchurch. He will take any necessary actions."

"OK. Fenchurch will run interference if needed."

"You'll take the case, then?" Brockington asked.

I had my doubts, but I needed the work. Five G's would do a lot for my bank balance.

"My rates are fifty dollars a day. I'll need an advance of two hundred for expenses."

"Fenchurch has a check for five hundred dollars prepared. That should cover the first week. Arrangements can be made for more if the matter takes longer. I'll expect an itemized list of expenses, but I won't object to anything reasonable. Do we have a deal, Mr. Tolliver?"

"We have a deal, Mr. Brockington." We shook on it, his grip being anything but limp. "Now if I could get some more details about this book?"

"Miss Lanier, here," indicating the school-marm, "can fill you in on the details and history of the book far better than I can. If you'll excuse me, I'm afraid my condition causes me to tire easily. I will leave you two alone now."

The attendant helped Brockington to his feet and he made his way painfully out the door by which he had entered.

"I'll have that check ready for you before you leave, Mr. Tolliver," Fenchurch said before following his employer from the study.

CHAPTER 3

"Just what is so special about this book, Miss Lanier? It is Miss, isn't it?" I asked once the others had left.

"It is Miss, Mr. Tolliver," she replied coldly. "Miss Abigail Lanier."

"Abigail," I remarked. "That's kind of an old fashioned name."

"I'm an old-fashioned kind of girl, Mr. Tolliver. But my friends call me Gail."

"I'll ask again, Gail, just what's so special about this book?"

"I didn't say that we were friends, Mr. Tolliver." She was trying to sound stern, but I could detect a touch of humor in her voice.

"Touché. But you still haven't answered my question. What is it that makes a book worth five G's?"

"It's worth far more than that, Mr. Tolliver. Mr. Brockington paid thirty-thousand for the Codex. That's not including the commission which he paid the dealer."

"OK. What makes this book worth thirty grand plus change?"

"Are you prepared for a bit of a lecture, Mr. Tolliver? That's the only way I can hope to explain it to you."

"It's been a while since I attended school, but shoot."

"To put it simply, the Rathcael Codex, that's the book's formal name, is a hand written manuscript in Latin, on velum with board covers covered in calf-skin. It's roughly ten inches by eight, and about an inch thick. It consists of one hundred and twenty eight leaves or pages."

"I follow you so far."

"As far as anyone knows, it was created by an Irish monk working somewhere in the west of Ireland during the late eleventh or early twelfth century. I don't know if you are familiar with the subject, but the Irish were masters at producing beautiful illuminated books.   In the best examples, the text, the margins, and the initial letters of chapters and paragraphs were elaborately decorated with colored inks or even gold leaf. The process was painstaking, all done by hand, of course, and it might take a monk years to produce a single volume."

"I'm aware of the concept, Miss Lanier," I responded. I didn't want her to think I was a total dummy. I actually had seen examples of illuminated manuscripts in a museum during the war. "And I can understand why such a book might be valuable to a collector.   But thirty thousand? These days that's a lot of cash.   Not to mention that someone was killed for it."

"Yes, well the Rathcael Codex is not just another illuminated manuscript, Mr. Toliver.   It is, as Mr. Brockington indicated, unique. Most illuminated books are religious   in   nature,   either   portions   of   the   bible, commentaries, or the lives of saints. This is not surprising considering where such books were produced. There are also some herbals, that is reference books about plants, and some of the classics and histories, that sort of thing. The Codex is none of these, and that's what makes it unique. To put it bluntly, the subject matter of the Codex deals with the sexual act, complete with illustrations."

"So we're talking about nine hundred year old pornography?"

"Oh, much more than just dirty pictures, Mr. Tolliver," she responded. "The monk that created the Codex was obsessed by sex, and not just in the physical, but in a metaphysical sense. From what I understand, he seemed to think that the path to salvation lay through the perfection of the sexual act. No one can understand how he was able to produce the Codex, which must have taken years, without incurring the censure of his superiors. By all rights, he probably should have been burned at the stake."

"You say from what you understand. I take it you haven't actually seen the book itself."

"Well, when the auction was announced, Mr. Brockington did send me to Europe to examine it. I and a select group of others were allowed to view the Codex opened to a single page, one of the milder ones, if the seller is to be believed. The seller, who chose to remain anonymous, was very concerned less the nature of the book get out. In many countries it would, indeed as you put it, be viewed as pornography. We were not allowed to look at more than that one page. A photographic copy of that page was provided to serious prospective buyers. I have a copy of that photograph here. It is roughly life size. Unfortunately, it is only in black and white."

She handed me an eight by ten print. I couldn't, of course, read the text. My Latin is a bit rusty and I never did have much exposure to medieval script. The picture at the top of the page, on the other hand, was only too comprehensible. I'd seen a copy once of what the owner had called the Kama Sutra. The print made that look like the Sunday comics. It's possible that I blushed. I certainly was noticing for the first time the faint scent of sandalwood coming from Miss Lanier.

I think I said something like, "I see."

"Mr. Brockington has no particular interest in the erotic content, Mr. Tolliver. His sole concern is in the unique nature and history of the Codex."

"History?" I asked, not so much because I cared, but because I wanted to hear more of Miss Lanier's voice.

"As you can imagine, over the years the Codex has passed through numerous hands. For several centuries it disappeared from sight, only to surface recently in one of the Balkan countries. I could give you more details, but I doubt if they would be of any help in recovering the Codex."

"Probably not. Mr. Brockington said that he used a dealer as an agent for the purchase."

"Yes. It's not at all unusual for intermediaries to be used in the procuring of rare art objects, both for purposes of security, and to keep the price down. In this case, given the nature of the Codex, Mr. Brockington also wanted to avoid undue publicity."

I didn't see the need to comment. If Brockington wanted to look at nine hundred year old dirty pictures that was his business.

"Just who was the go between?"

"His name was David Levi. He is the murdered man. He owns—owned a bookstore dealing in rare and antique volumes. He was quite well known and respected in the trade. Mr. Brockington had had dealings with him over the years, so it was only natural that when the Codex came up for sale that he chose to involve Mr. Levi."

"And just what were the arrangements? I assume it wasn't just sent by parcel post."

"Mr. Levi purchased the book with funds provided by Mr. Brockington. Mr. Brockington's name was not used, but I suspect that the seller had a good idea as to who the purchaser was. The Codex was transported by a bonded courier, an employee of a London firm that specializes in this sort of thing. He delivered the Codex to Mr. Levi last night. Levi called to confirm that the Codex had arrived. He was supposed to deliver it today but—"

"—But somebody bumped him off and swiped the book," I completed.

"I wouldn't have put it quite so colorfully, but, yes, that is what happened."

"Just how many people knew about the codex and the shipping arrangements?"

"Mr. Brockington, Mr. Fenchurch, myself, the courier. And Mr. Levi, of course."

"Of course."

"No one else? Mr. Brockington's lawyer or banker perhaps?"

"I don't believe so. They are quite used to Mr. Brockington spending large sums for books and other antiquities, so there wouldn't have been anything out of the ordinary in his transferring substantial funds to Mr. Levi."

"I see."

"I'm not sure what you're implying, Mr. Tolliver," Miss Lanier said huffily.

"I'm not implying anything about you personally, Miss Lanier. It's just that art theft, or in this case, book theft, is rarely a random act. Burglars tend to go after hard cash or stuff like jewelry which they can fence easily. They wouldn't be likely to grab a book in a language they couldn't read, even if it did have pretty pictures. Somebody knew about this codex thing and that it had arrived at Levi's."

"Yes, of course. I understand." I wasn't sure she did, but then most people get nervous when they discover that they are a suspect for theft—and murder. "Is there anything else you'd like to know, Mr. Tolliver?"

"I do have one more question, Miss Lanier?"

"What is that?"

"How certain are you that this codex is the real deal? That it's not a forgery of some sort? Famous paintings are faked all the time, why not a book?"

"Oh, I think that would be highly unlikely, Mr. Tolliver. To even attempt to create a forgery on this scale would involve way too much work. It would literally have taken years of painstaking labor. Even for thirty thousand dollars I don't think that it would be worth the trouble."

"I'll have to take your word for that, Miss Lanier."

"If there is nothing else, then, Mr. Tolliver, I'll go see if Mr. Fenchurch has that check ready for you."

Evidently, Fenchurch had the check ready, because he appeared almost immediately carrying a check in his hand. From the tight grip he held on it, I wasn't sure that he was going to give it up. I sensed that the secretary didn't approve of Brockington's hiring a private detective. There was an awkward moment of silence before he reluctantly handed the check over.

I took a quick gander at it. Everything seemed in order.

"I hate to mention this, Mr. Fenchurch, but it's going to take a few days for a check of this size to clear at my bank. I'm not doubting that it's good, mind you. It's just that I know Mr. Brockington wants me to get working on this case right away, and it would help if I had some cash to cover expenses."

"Really, Mr. Tolliver—" Fenchurch objected, then thought better of it. "Would fifty dollars be sufficient?"

"That would be adequate," I conceded.

"Very well." He pulled out his wallet and counted out a pair of double sawbucks and a couple of fins. He looked as if he was going to say something before handing the money over, but he didn't.

"I can give you a receipt if you like," I said as I stashed the cash in my wallet.

"That won't be necessary, Mr. Tolliver. I'll just add it to my accounts. I will be auditing your expense reports when you turn them in."

"I'll keep that in mind, Fenchurch. I think I can find my own way out."

That was probably true, but Jeeves was waiting at the study door to escort me off the premises.

I had to walk a couple of blocks uphill to find a cab, but I didn't mind. With a check for half a grand in my pocket I was in a pretty good mood, and the dough I had extracted from Fenchurch meant I would be able to pay off the cabbie.

Chapter 4

First thing in the morning I went to the bank and deposited the check. The teller looked at it suspiciously, but he must have decided it was genuine. He assured me that the funds would be available in a few days. Until then, I would have to get by on the cash Fenchurch had slipped me.

I had a lot riding on solving this case, so I needed to get to work on it fast. The more time that passed, the greater was the chance that the codex would vanish into obscurity yet again.

I placed a call to police headquarters and asked for Lt. Miller.

"Miller speaking," the voice was gruff, the accent vaguely Midwestern.

"This is James Tolliver. You've probably heard that I've been hired by Brockington to find this missing book of his. He said that he had arranged for the cooperation of the department."

"Yeah, I heard." Miller didn't sound too happy about the prospect.

"Look, Al, I'm not trying to step on any toes, but I've got a job to do, same as you."

"What do you want, Tolliver?" His answer was more resignation than agreement.

"I'd like to look over the crime scene if that's possible. I know you've got a homicide investigation going, but I figure the crime scene boys must be finished with their act by now—"

"All right. I can meet you there in a half hour," Miller interrupted curtly. "You know the address?"

"Yeah. I'll be there."

I found myself talking to a dead phone.

David Levi's bookstore was at 843 Stevenson a block south of Market St. It was only a few blocks from my office, so I decided to hoof it even if that did mean pulling the collar of my trenchcoat up around my neck. There was a damp breeze coming off the bay, but at least it had blown off the fog.

When I got to the address, there was a bored looking patrolman standing in front of the shop. The shop itself was about what you'd expect; a couple of dusty windows sporting the words "Levi's Used Books" in faded gold leaf. Inside the windows were a number of books opened in display. It didn't look as if Levi had gone in for best sellers or any other form of popular fiction for that matter.

The cop looked at me suspiciously as I approached, but his manner changed when I asked if Miller had arrived yet.

"You must be Tolliver, the private dick. The lieutenant is inside. He said to let you by."

"Thanks."

He stepped aside to let me by. I went through the door into the gloom of the shop. The place had that peculiar musty smell that you only get from moldy paper. Shelves that ran nearly to the ceiling were set perpendicular to a central aisle along the length of the narrow shop. If there was any order to the books stacked on them, I couldn't spot it, but I did see a lot of calfskin bindings and gold leaf titles. The only illumination other than what seeped in through the front windows came from a trio of globes suspended from the ceiling over the aisle.

"You in here, Al?"

"That you, Tolliver? I'm in the back."

I followed the central aisle towards the rear of the shop where a small office had been carved out by a partition that went up just short of the ceiling. Inside was a roll-top desk of ancient vintage, a wooden swivel chair and a table piled high with books. For that matter, every flat surface in the store was covered with stacks of books. In the corner next to the desk was an old key operated safe from the last century.

Miller was poking through the cubbyholes of the desk when he saw me. The lieutenant was a burly six-foot two with graying brown hair that was thinning at the top. His ancestors had been Germans who had settled in some burg east of the Mississippi sometime in the last century. He'd come west before the war and become a cop when he couldn't find honest work. He wasn't a bad guy to work with, but you didn't want to get on the wrong side of him.

"This is where he was found," Miller said, pointing to the floor in front of the safe. In the dim light I could see what was left of a pool of blood. "He'd been shot in the back of the head at close range by a small caliber pistol. They weren't able to find a shell casing, but it was probably an automatic. A .22 or a .25. Know for sure when the autopsy is done. The doc said he'd been killed sometime between ten the previous night and four yesterday morning."

"Who found the body?"

"A customer who had an appointment at ten yesterday morning. I gather such arrangements weren't unusual. When he found the door locked, he got concerned and talked to the beat cop who happened to know that the place next door had a spare key so they could take in parcels if any arrived when Levi wasn't there. The officer used the key and found Levi lying dead in front of the safe."

"Any sign of a break-in?"

"No. No scratches on the front door. The rear door probably hasn't been opened in years."

"So Levi likely knew the killer?"

"Well enough to let him in. From what the neighbor said, Levi didn't keep regular hours. Customers sometimes came in well into the evening."

"Was the safe open or closed when the body was found?"

"Closed," Miller said succinctly.

"Have you tried to open it?" I asked.

"Levi had a key for it on his key chain."

Miller produced a large key from his pocket and proceeded to insert it in the keyhole of the safe. He gave it a couple of turns and then pushed down on the handle. The heavy metal door swung open. Inside I could see a cash box and what looked to be a couple of ledgers. There were also a number of books on the lower shelves. Unlike the stock in the front of the shop, these were all stacked neatly.

"Anything missing? Other than the codex, I mean."

"Look at the place," Miller said with disgust. "The only one that could have told us that is Levi, and he's dead. I can tell you this, there is nearly eight hundred bucks in that cash box. This wasn't some random robbery. The killer came for one thing and one thing only."

"From what you've told me, the killer was someone Levi knew. Levi let him in late at night, probably because he had an appointment. They go back here to the office. Then, while Levi opens the safe, the killer pops him one in the back of the head. He grabs what he wants, presumably the codex, then locks up the safe and leaves, turning out the lights and locking the front door."

"That's about the size of it," Miller agreed. "Except there's nothing to prove that the killer was a man. A small gun like that—fits in a purse. It could have easily been a woman."

"I suppose so, though most of the women I know go in for jewelry, not old books," I commented. As I said that, it occurred to me that I knew of at least one woman for whom that wasn't the case.

"Tell me, Tolliver," Miller asked, "just what is it about this book that makes it so valuable? That makes it worth killing someone for?"

I'd been gazing at the stain on the floor, but I looked up at Miller. The lieutenant is no dummy, but his idea of culture is drinking a beer while listening to a ball game on the radio.

"I don't know that much about it, but the codex, and that's what it's called, the Rathcael Codex, isn't a printed book. It's a handwritten manuscript created by some Irish monk nine hundred or so years ago. From what I've been told, it's unique, a one of a kind item. Just the sort of thing a rich collector would pay big bucks for. In this case, thirty-thousand of them. In my book, for a lot of people, that's enough reason to kill for.

Miller gave a low whistle. "Who'd a thought—"

"Yeah."

"But how'd you go about fencing something like that?" Like I said, Miller is smarter than he looks.

"My guess is the killer has a buyer already lined up. Some other collector with too much money. The problem is that they could be anywhere in the world."

Miller thought about that for a moment, then shrugged. "Have you seen enough?"

"Yeah. At least for now. Will you let me see the autopsy report when you get it?"

"As soon as I get it. I've been told to cooperate fully. And Jim, I expect that to be a two way street. If you come across anything, I want you to let me know about it. After all, I've got a murder to solve."

Miller didn't use my first name often. When he did, I knew he was being serious.

"Don't worry. My interest is in the book, but if I find the book, I'll probably have found the killer. I'll let you know when I do."

"You do that. Let's get out of here. These old books are making my hay fever act up." To emphasize that point, Miller pulled a handkerchief out of his hip pocket and loudly blew his nose.

As I headed up Mason St. back to my office, I had a lot to think about. It was pretty obvious that the robbery of Levi's bookstore hadn't been a random act, it had been an inside job. The killer had known that the codex would be there. Furthermore, Levi had to have known the killer, known him—or her—well enough to stay late in the shop to let them in, and while it was possible the killer had forced the old man to open his safe at gun point, I was betting that Levi had known the killer well enough to turn his back on him.

If it had been an inside job, the number of suspects was pretty limited. Assuming that Levi himself hadn't let slip the fact that the codex had arrived, there were only three people that I knew of who had had that bit of information, Brockington, Fenchurch, and Miss Lanier. I was pretty sure that I could rule out Brockington. He didn't have a motive. He'd already paid out some thirty grand for the book, and certainly had nothing to gain by stealing it. Fenchurch seemed a more likely suspect. I'd pretty much taken an instant dislike to the secretary, and not just because of his affectations and pretensions. He just wasn't the sort of man

I'd put my trust in. As for Miss Lanier, well, I was finding it hard to think anything ill of her.

Of course, there was the courier, whoever that had been. He had delivered the package to Levi, so he would have known it was there. But had he been aware of what had been in the package? I didn't know the answer to that question, but it was a lead to follow up on.

Lost in thought as I was, I hadn't been paying much attention to my surroundings, but I had a feeling that I was being followed. At the next street corner I paused for a moment to look around. I didn't notice anything obvious, no one making a point of staring at a shop window or looking anywhere but in my direction. The only thing out of the ordinary was the black figure of a Catholic priest about half a block down the street, but he was strolling along as if he didn't have a care in the world.

I chalked the feeling up to my imagination and being on edge. I was also hungry. I decided that what I needed was a beer and some lunch, and I headed for a nearby saloon that offered both.

CHAPTER 5

I emerged from the bar refreshed by a beer and a corned beef sandwich, and in a better frame of mind. That didn't stop me from taking a quick glance around when I hit the street, but if someone was tailing me, they were doing a pretty good job of it because nothing attracted my attention.

Satisfied that I wasn't being followed, I thought about my next move. One problem with stealing something like the codex or any serious piece of art is disposing of it. With jewelry, that's not so much of a problem; precious stones can be unmounted, diamonds can be recut, gold or silver can be melted down so as to be untraceable. But how did one go about fencing a stolen book, particularly a one of a kind item such as the codex? I doubted that the killer was working directly with the eventual buyer. It was much more likely that there was an intermediary involved. The question was who? I didn't have much experience with literary theft; that was outside of the circles I ran in, but I did have an idea of someone who might have a clue.

Alexei Andreavich is a Russian émigré who has a small antiques store on Geary. Like a lot of White Russians, Alexei migrated to Shanghai after the Reds took over. Unlike a lot of them, Alexei managed to get out while the getting was good and ended up in San Francisco with enough money to set himself up in business. He mostly deals in antique furniture, but he dabbles in paintings and icons as well. As far as I know, Alexei comes by most of his stock honestly, but he also doesn't ask awkward questions when people try to sell things. I'd run into him trying to track down a stolen statue. He hadn't been involved, but he'd had a good idea of who might have been, and had slipped me the information. Since then, I've cultivated the relationship.

I could tell that Alexei wasn't too happy to see me, but he greeted me cordially anyway.

"James. I haven't seen you in some time. You are well, I trust?" His English was fluent but the accent was indefinable, part British, part French, part who knows what. His mother had been English, his father supposedly some lesser Russian nobility. He was a smallish man, with just enough hair to comb over the balding spot on the top of his head. His suit was well tailored but of a cut twenty years out of date. A pair of pince-nez glasses dangled from a black ribbon hung around his neck.

"Alexei. How's business?"

"If you must ask, James, it's terrible. No one appreciates quality anymore. It's all chrome and brushed nickel these days. It makes it hard for a poor business man like me to survive."

"Times are tough all over," I agreed. "But speaking of old things, that's what I wanted to pick your brain over."

Alexei looked intrigued but cautious.

"What are you trying to track down now, James?"

"A book."

"A book?" Alexei exclaimed in surprise. "There's no money in books. Especially old ones. Do you see any books in here?" he said waving his hand around at the contents of the cramped shop. "That's because there is no market for books."

"Well, there might be for this one. It's quite old and valuable."

"Oh?" Alexei's ears pricked up. "You interest me, James. You must tell me more."

"It's an illuminated manuscript. Irish. Eleventh century. About so big." I indicated with my hands the dimensions as Miss Lanier had described them to me me.

"It sounds as if it should be in a museum," Alexei commented.

"Probably. But it was stolen the night before last. A man was killed in the process. David Levi. Did you know him?"

"Sure. I know—I knew Levi. He bought and sold old books. A decent man, but not much of a head for business. A lot of his trade was to people buying books by the yard to fill shelves to make other people think they were intelligent. Nice bindings, gold lettering on the spine, who cares what's inside. All for show. But he did deal in some real rarities, as well. He also acted as agent for some wealthy collectors. I've never heard of him being mixed up in anything crooked, though."

"I didn't say he was. Like you say, he was acting as an agent for my client in the purchase of this particular book. Someone killed him to get their hands on it."

"Too bad. He was a decent man for a Jew. But what has this to do with me?"

"I'm trying to recover the book that was taken. My problem is that I haven't got any idea as to who the fences are for an item like that. I was hoping you might."

"Not really my line, James. As you know, I'm an honest man. But tell me more about this—book."

"It's called the Rathcael Codex. It's worth at least thirty grand. It's been in and out of circulation for the last few hundred years. From what I've been told, the subject matter is, well, out of the ordinary."

Alexei raised his eyebrow.

"Let's just say that it has some dirty pictures in it."

Alexei burst out laughing. "Nine hundred year old smut! I like it, James. I'm not sure I can help you much, though. I don't think that there's anyone in San Francisco that would deal in something like that. The market is too specialized, too limited. There are probably fewer than a couple of dozen collectors in the world that would be interested. My guess would be that the intermediary, and I'm sure there is one, is someone from out of town, New York maybe, or more likely London or Rome. The thief might be from out of town, too."

"I'm not so sure of that, Alexei. Levi knew whoever killed him, knew him at least well enough to let him into his shop late at night."

"I can see you have some ideas along those lines, James."

"Yeah, but nothing like any proof."

"Sorry I couldn't be of more help. I wasn't friends with Levi, but as I said, he was a decent old man. He never harmed anyone. All he was interested in were his books. It is a shame he was killed, though."

"Yeah," I said. I slipped a sawbuck onto the counter between us. "If you should hear anything, Alexei, let me know. There'll be something in it for you if it pans out."

"I'll be sure to keep my ears open, James."

As I walked out of Alexei's shop I unconsciously checked around for signs of a tail, but if there was one, I couldn't spot him. I was so spooked that I even found myself keeping an eye open for the Catholic priest I had seen earlier.

My talk with Alexei had confirmed what I had already suspected, the market for something like the codex was extremely limited and none of the local fences were likely to have been involved. It probably would be a waste of my time to pursue that line of inquiry. If the intermediary or broker was from out of town, the only way I'd stumble across them would be by pure blind luck.

I had a feeling that the same would hold true for the usual burglary suspects. It was unlikely that any of them had been involved. If they had, they would have taken more than just the codex, if only to cover up the fact that the codex had been the target of the robbery.

No, the killer had been an amateur, a clever one, but still an amateur. The execution of the crime had been slick enough. There had been the use of a small caliber automatic for one, the report from the single shot wouldn't have been loud and would have been muffled further by the piles of books lining the shop. If anyone had heard it, they would probably have just written it off as a firecracker or a car backfire.

There was the fact, too, that Levi had let the killer in after hours, so there was none of the fuss and muss of a break-in or the complications of trying to get the safe open. It had been an old model, but still, nothing that an amateur could open easily without the key. Getting Levi to open the safe himself had made the theft quick and clean. The whole business had probably only taken a few minutes.

But the killer might have been a little too clever. One thing was clear, Levi had known the person who had murdered him. That was why the old man had been killed, because he would have been able to identify the person who took the codex.

All this thinking brought me back to my earlier conclusion, namely that it had been an inside job. And that brought me back to Fenchurch as the prime suspect. I had a feeling that Brockington's secretary would be the key to finding the codex.

As I opened the lobby door to my building I ran into a black clothed figure coming out.

"Padre," I said, holding the door open for the clergyman.

"Thank you, my son," he replied calmly before walking away down the street.

I hadn't gotten a close enough look at the priest I had seen earlier to tell if this was the same man. They were both roughly the same size, but then there was nothing unusual about that as they had both been average in height and medium build. It was probably just a coincidence, I thought, as there must be dozens of priests in San Francisco that fit that description. Only my overactive imagination had caused me to take notice.

.

CHAPTER 6

When I got up to my office I called Brockington's house. The butler answered, at least from the snooty accent I assumed it was the butler, and asked for Fenchurch. I didn't particularly want to speak to the secretary, but I did want to know if he was around.

"Whom may I say is calling, sir?" the butler asked.

"This is James Tolliver, the detective your boss hired," I replied, hoping I wouldn't get the run around.

"Mr. Tolliver. I've been instructed that any calls from you be directed to Miss Lanier. Would that be acceptable, sir?"

"Suits me just fine."

"Very good sir. If you will wait a moment, I will see if Miss Lanier is available."

I was going to say, "Thanks," but Jeeves had set the receiver down before I got the chance. Not quite two minutes later I heard it being picked up again.

"Mr. Tolliver, don't tell me that you've made progress already." There was a note of skepticism in Miss Lanier's voice.

"Not exactly, Miss Lanier. Though I assure you I have been on the job. I've examined the scene of the crime, talked to some connections of mine—"

"I didn't mean to imply that I doubted your work ethic, Mr. Tolliver," Miss Lanier interrupted.

"It doesn't matter to me whether you do or not, Miss Lanier. I'm used to getting paid for results, not promises. But I was hoping that either you or Mr. Fenchurch could help me out with some information."

"I'll provide any help I can, Mr. Tolliver. What is it you want to know?"

"Well, it's like this, Miss Lanier, the way I figure it, something like this codex will be hard for the thief or thieves to dispose of. Would I be right in thinking that the market for a book of that nature would be fairly limited?"

"I think that would be a fair statement, Mr. Tolliver." She seemed amused by my question.

"That's what I thought. I asked around to some of my contacts and they confirmed my assumption."

"I hope you were discrete, Mr. Tolliver," Miss Lanier commented sharply.

"I'm always discrete, Miss Lanier. But getting back to my original point, I'm thinking that the people most likely to be in the market for the codex would be the ones who bid for it in the original auction, the one in which Mr. Brockington acquired it. I was wondering if it would be possible for you to provide me with a list of those who participated."

"A complete list would be difficult to compile, Mr. Tolliver. You have to understand that many of the principals dealt through agents to preserve their anonymity, much as Mr. Brockington did."

"So the other bidders wouldn't have known that your employer was one of the bidders or that he had the winning bid?"

"No, most of them wouldn't have access to that information, though I would think that many of them would have had their suspicions. The collectors of manuscripts of that value are a rather rarified and limited group, Mr. Tolliver, and the members know of most of the others."

"I see. Maybe I'm asking the wrong question then, Miss Lanier. Would it be possible for you to come up with a list of potential buyers? If I knew who was interested, I might be able to spot them if they show up in town."

"That sounds reasonable, Mr. Tolliver. I can't give you that information off the top of my head, but I should be able to create a list of likely buyers and send it over to your office by messenger if that would be acceptable?"

"That would be eminently acceptable, Miss Lanier," I replied.

"I should be able to have it for you by this evening, then."

"Thanks. That would be swell. Say, the butler said that he had been told that any calls from me should be directed to you. Does that mean I should be working with you rather than Fenchurch?"

"Do you have a problem with that, Mr. Tolliver?"

"Not at all, Miss Lanier. You're much more my type. I'd rather talk to you than Fenchurch any day. I was just wondering if there was any particular reason such as him being out of town or something."

"No, he's here in the house right now working with Mr. Brockington. It's just that I think Mr. Brockington thought it would be more efficient if there was a single point of contact, and seeing as I am more knowledgeable when it comes to the codex he felt it would be most productive if you dealt with me."

"I understand, Miss Lanier, and I didn't mean to insinuate anything—"

"Oh, I doubt that, Mr. Tolliver," she interrupted, sounding amused.

"Touché again, Miss Lanier."

"Will there be anything else, Mr. Tolliver?"

"No, that should do it for the moment."

"I'll have that list to you this evening, then. Good-bye, Mr. Tolliver."

The line went dead before I could respond.

I called down to a garage that lets me rent cars at a reasonable rate. They usually aren't new, but they are cheap and they do run, which was the important thing. The owner of the garage said he could fix me up with something. I told him I'd be there in half an hour to pick it up.

Forty-five minutes later I was parked down the street from Brockington's in a spot that gave me a good view of the front door. It was just after three in the afternoon. By six, I was getting hungry and debating whether to pack it in for the day and return the car when a taxi pulled up in front of the house. After about a minute the front door opened and Fenchurch came out. He was wearing a worn overcoat and a battered fedora that seemed out of keeping with the sharp way he had been dressed when I had seen him earlier in the day. Fenchurch got into the waiting cab and after a moment it took off.

I started the car and followed. The car was a five year old Chevrolet coupe with a dull black paint job; just the sort of vehicle for tailing someone, common and unostentatious enough to be unremarkable.

The trip wasn't a long one, and ended up in front of a large Victorian house on Russian Hill. I pulled over to the curb a few houses away. Fenchurch got out of the cab and paid off the driver. After the cab had gone, he walked a few houses up the street and crossed over to another house with a small yard surrounded by a high wrought-iron fence. After looking both ways, Fenchurch opened the gate and went up the steps to the front door. They seemed to be expecting him, because the door opened almost immediately and admitted Brockington's secretary.

I wasn't sure if Fenchurch was trying to conceal anything or not. The cab had taken a more or less direct route to the destination. The fact that it had stopped a few houses down might mean something or it might not. Cabbie's do make mistakes. As to the old coat and hat, it just might mean that given the weather, Fenchurch hadn't wanted to wear his best.

I shut the engine off and waited. After five minutes, Fenchurch hadn't come out. I got out of the car, crossed over to the other side of the street and strolled down the block trying to look casual. I wanted to get a closer look at the house.

It wasn't as nice as the one that the cab had stopped in front of to let Fenchurch out. It was a big place in the Queen Anne style, three stories, with a turret sticking out on one corner of the front. It needed some paint and what landscaping there was in the tiny yard was overgrown and in need of some tender love and care. Any lights that were on inside were concealed by heavy drapes on the windows.

As I passed the gate, I noticed a small brass plaque attached to it. The engraving on it read "Temple of Transcendental Enlightenment."

Now San Francisco has its share of cults and religious crackpots, probably more so than most cities. It seems to attract them. I'd never heard of the "Temple of Transcendental Enlightenment" but then I didn't go in for that sort of thing. I hadn't thought Fenchurch, whatever his faults, would have either, but then I didn't really know the man very well.

I strolled to the end of the block, crossed back to the other side of the street, and walked back to the car. It was about a half an hour before Fenchurch came out. Evidently he hadn't called for a cab. I started the car and followed him over to Hyde St. where he waited to get on a cable car heading up the hill.

Following a cable car and not getting spotted isn't easy to do. I'm not sure that I managed it, but I was still keeping up when I saw Fenchurch get off. If he was worried about being tailed, he wasn't showing it. From the cable car line, he headed west. Ten minutes later, he walked up the front steps of Brockington's house. Evidently he had a key, because he didn't bother to ring for the butler, letting himself in.

I doubted that Fenchurch would be going out again that night, so I drove back to the garage and turned the car in. When the owner looked it over, he seemed surprised that it wasn't sporting any new bullet holes, but then he has some exaggerated notion of what my business is like from reading too many cheap detective magazines.

When I got back to the office, I found an envelope that had been slipped in through the mail slot in the door. It had my name on it in a prim, feminine hand. When I opened it, inside was the list that Miss Lanier had promised me.

The list was as precisely organized as if it had been composed on a typewriter, but it had been written by hand in the same elegant penmanship that had been used on the envelope.

The list itself was short, which wasn't surprising. Just how many people were there who would be willing to spend thirty grand on a book, no matter how old and rare it was? In addition to the names, Miss Lanier had added a brief biographical note for each person and a comment as to how likely the person would be to use extreme measures to obtain the codex. There was only one name on the list that I recognized, an American, the heir to one of the eastern railroad fortunes. The others included a Brit, a Swede, and a Frenchman, all wealthy in a quiet sort of way, and at least according to Miss Lanier, unlikely to be involved in anything illegal. There were two other names on the list about which Miss Lanier was less sure on that point, a man who claimed to be a Hungarian count and a shadowy figure who might or might not be a Turk. Miss Lanier had added a postscript saying that she thought that there were several other parties that had been involved in the bidding but whose identity she was unsure of.

None of this looked particularly promising as a lead, but I would have to check them out as best I could. In the morning. I turned out the lights, locked up the office and headed for the elevator.

Chapter 7

It was a little after eight when I left the office for my apartment. The kind of fog that San Francisco is famous for had settled in for the night. I pulled up the collar of my overcoat and started walking home.

I'd gone less than a block when I noticed a shadowy, black figure at the point where the fog became a wall of gray. He was walking in the same direction I was. Running into the same priest twice might be a coincidence, but not three times. I turned at the corner to see if he would do the same. He did.

The figure of a priest isn't something you are supposed to be afraid of, but then, the priests aren't supposed to be in the business of tailing people. I turned at the next corner and found a dark alley to duck into. There wasn't much traffic about, and I could hear the footsteps of the priest. They slowed when he turned the corner and couldn't see me, but they came on, just the same.

I waited until he had gone past the alley and then came up behind him. I wasn't carrying a gun, I don't normally unless I'm expecting trouble, but a knuckle in the back will convince most people. The priest stopped and raised his hands. Unlike most people in that situation, he didn't protest, instead he waited for me to say the first word.

I patted him down with my left hand. In the pocket of his cassock I found a gun, a German Luger, which I relieved him of.

"Curious thing for a priest to be carrying around, don't you think, padre?"

"We live in dangerous times, Mr. Tolliver." There was more than a hint of an Irish brogue in his accent. He also knew my name.

"Still, I think I'll keep this for the moment." I stuffed the pistol into the left pocket of my overcoat. I put my right hand, the one that had been pretending to be gun, in the other pocket.

"As you wish. You seem to have the advantage of me for the moment."

"Why don't you turn around? I like to see who I'm talking to."

"As do I," the priest said turning to face me. He'd let his hands drop, but he kept them where I could see them. He had a thin weathered face with a sharp nose on which perched a pair of gold-rimmed glasses. He was dressed in a traditional cassock complete with broad-brimmed black hat. He seemed to be contemplating me with some amusement. "Just what would you be liking to talk about, my son?"

"I guess first of all I'd like to know if you really are a priest, or is the outfit just a dodge?"

"Oh, I assure you, Mr. Tolliver, I am a priest."

"Then I guess I'd like to know why a priest would be following me?"

"Might I suggest, then, that we find someplace with a bit more privacy to discuss the matter, preferably someplace warmer and drier. If I had wanted someplace cold and damp I could have stayed in Ireland."

"Fair enough. My office is just around the corner. But then you knew that, didn't you?"

"I confess that I did." For someone who had been caught out and knew he was facing someone with a gun, the priest was playing it very cool.

In our little game of follow the leader, we had walked around three sides of the block my building was on. Completing the circuit of the block we found ourselves back in the lobby. As we rode the elevator up to my office, the priest said, "You can stop pretending that your knuckle is a gun, Mr. Tolliver. It must be getting tiring."

I pulled my hand out of the pocket, letting it relax. I unlocked the door to my office and ushered the priest inside.

"Have a seat, padre," I said, motioning to a chair in front of my desk. I hung up my hat and overcoat on the coat rack after removing the Luger. I set the pistol on the top of the desk just out of reach of the padre.

"You wouldn't have a drop of something warming, would you? I admit of late I've grown accustomed to warmer climes."

"I'm afraid all I can offer you is rye, padre."

"Oh, that's quite alright, Mr. Tolliver. I assure you my tastes are quite catholic." He seemed amused by his little joke.

I dug out a bottle and a couple of glasses from the lower left hand desk drawer and set them on the table.

"Help yourself, padre."

"Bless you, my son." The priest poured a couple of fingers of the amber liquid into his glass, enough to feel the liquor, but not as much as a drunk would have poured. I poured the same amount in the other glass.

"Slange," the priest toasted, then took a slip of his glass.

"Now just who the hell are you, padre?"

"My name, Mr. Tolliver, is Father Ignatius Donnelly. I am an agent of the Curia in Rome. I can show you my credentials, if you'd like?"

He reached into an inner pocket of his cassock and produced a passport like document which he handed over. I opened it up. It was quite impressive looking, full of seals and things. It was also in Latin. I did recognize Donnelly's name and the words "Vatican" and "Curia."

"I'm afraid I'm a protestant, padre. I don't read much Latin."

"I assure you it's genuine enough. It confirms that I am an ordained priest and in the employ of the foreign service of the Vatican. As I said, I am an agent of the Curia."

My curiosity was getting the better of me. "I wasn't aware that the Vatican had agents. Just what does that entail and how does one become a papal agent?"

"It's rather a long story, Mr. Tolliver."

"I've got the time, and there's still liquor in the bottle."

"Very well, I've no objection. In my misspent youth I was involved with the republican cause in Ireland. After the Easter rebellion failed, it became necessary for me to leave the country. I took sanctuary in a seminary in Italy, one that welcomes Irishmen no matter what their pasts. While there, I found my true vocation, as it were. In due time, I was ordained and became a priest."

"An interesting story, padre, but it doesn't really explain the Luger."

The padre paused for a moment and sipped his whiskey. "There I was, an Irish priest who, because of his past, couldn't go home to Ireland. I might have ended up a missionary in Africa or a parish priest in America, but someone in the Curia took notice of my past. I'm not proud of what I did back then, but I was good at what I did and I had acquired certain skills—"

"Like how to shoot a Luger?" I interjected.

"Like how to shoot a Luger. Amongst others. Somewhat to my surprise, I must say, I found that the Curia sometimes has need of such skills. I was offered a position.

Considering the source of the offer, it wasn't a post which I could refuse."

"Just what does an agent of the Curia do, padre?"

"Oh, various things. Anything where the conventional means have failed or would be ineffective. Sometimes it involves assuring the security of various members of the Church's hierarchy, sometimes it involves recovering church property that has been lost or misappropriated. Which brings me to my purpose for being in San Francisco."

"Let me guess. It involves the Rathcael Codex."

"Precisely, Mr. Tolliver."

"Just what claim does the Vatican have on the codex? My client appears to have purchased it legitimately."

"That may be true, Mr. Tolliver, but the seller didn't have the right to sell it. The codex is rightfully the property of the Vatican Library."

"From what I understand of the subject matter of the book, I would have thought that the codex was a little risqué for the Vatican Library."

"You have to understand, Mr. Tolliver, that the manuscript was created in a monastery. As such, it comes under the purview of the Vatican. When the Vatican became aware of the existence of the codex, it took steps to acquire it in order to prevent the dissemination of the contents—"

"In other words, they wanted to suppress the codex?" I interrupted.

"There are a great number of books in the Vatican Library to which access is restricted, either because of errors in doctrine, because they would bring the Church into disrepute, or for reasons of politics. That is not a matter for me to decide or debate, Mr. Tolliver. I am only following the instructions of my superiors."

"So the Vatican Library had the codex at one time. How did it come to misplace it?"

"It was checked out by one of the Borgias in the early 1500's."

"Lucretia?"

"No, her father, Pope Alexander VI. Evidently he took an interest in the subject matter. Unfortunately, in the confusion following his untimely death, the codex was misplaced and not returned to the Library. The Vatican has been seeking to recover it ever since."

"Four hundred years is a long time to be looking for something, padre."

"Yes, it is. That's why, when it was learned that the manuscript had surfaced an attempt was made to purchase it. Unfortunately, at the time, the Vatican's agent was outbid. When it was learned that Mr. Brockington was the purchaser, I was sent here to try to obtain it from him."

"By fair means or foul?"

"By fair means, Mr. Tolliver. I was instructed to approach Brockington and persuade him to part with the codex, even purchase it if necessary, or, failing that, try to obtain possession through the courts. However, since Mr. Levi was murdered and the codex stolen, those plans have changed. Now I'm trying to track down and recover the codex by any legal means possible."

"Which brings us back to the question, why have you been following me?"

"Because, Mr. Tolliver, I judged that the most efficient means to obtain my end. You are much more familiar with San Francisco than I am, and I believe your chances of success in locating the codex to be much higher than that of the local constabulary."

"Thanks for that vote of confidence, but I don't have the codex, and why would I give it to you even if I had it? I already have a client and five thousand reasons why I shouldn't."

"I understand completely, Mr. Tolliver. You are a man of ethics, which is why I have tried to appeal to your sense of justice. I can see, though, that that will not work. In that case, I will just have to deal with Mr. Brockington when and if you recover the codex."

"Fair enough."

"I must warn you, though, Mr. Tolliver, that if I get to the codex first, my instructions are clear."

"As are mine," I responded.

"Then we understand each other, don't we? I thank you for the whiskey. Mr. Tolliver. If I could trouble you for the return of my pistol—"

I looked the priest in the eye, and decided that he wasn't going to shoot me, at least not yet. I slid the pistol across the desk. He picked it up and dropped it in the pocket of his cassock.

"Good night, Mr. Tolliver."

"Good night, padre."

With that, the priest left. I finished the whiskey that was left in my glass and started home.

CHAPTER 8

I made a detour on the way home. There was a piece of information that I wanted, and I had a feeling I wasn't going to get it by reading the newspapers or heading to the library. Both of those can be a gold mine for a detective, but they are selective in the kind of pay dirt they contain.

There was someone I knew that might have the dope I was looking for, a reporter for the *Chronicle* named Shorty Smith. Like most of the reporters I know, Smith liked an occasional drink, and this time of night he was as liable to be found in a dive bar across the street from the paper's offices as anywhere else, so I headed in that direction.

The bar wasn't much, but being so close to the *Chronicle* building it didn't have to be. It was a long, narrow room on the ground floor of the building a couple of steps down from the sidewalk. The bar ran the length of one side with four small booths along the other for any patrons who wanted a semblance of privacy. The lighting was dim, the air thick with cigarette smoke and filled with the buzz of voices and the clinking of glasses. I spotted Shorty nursing a double towards the far end of the bar. He was talking to a couple of other newspaper men that I halfway recognized.

Why Smith got saddled with a nickname like Shorty I'll never know except perhaps for the alliteration. He was just short of six feet, skinny, and had thinning hair that at one point had been pale blonde. He was dressed just like you'd imagine a reporter would be dressed in a cheap suit that needed a pressing. He was so engrossed in the conversation he was having that he didn't notice me until I leaned on the bar next to him.

"Can I buy you a drink, Shorty?"

He turned to look in my direction and smiled. I wasn't sure if he was pleased to see me or it was the offer of a free drink. The newspapermen he'd been talking to looked interested, but didn't say anything.

"James. It's been awhile. I won't refuse. The drink, that is."

I caught the eye of the bartender, signaled for a refill for Shorty and the same for myself and then dropped a couple of bucks on the bar. The bartender grabbed a bottle of bourbon from the backbar and a second glass and poured a couple of fingers of whiskey into each.

"To what do I owe the pleasure, James?" Shorty said raising his glass to me.

"I've got some questions, Shorty. I thought you might have the answers."

"I'm intrigued, if not surprised. I didn't expect the whiskey to come gratis. Shall we adjourn to my office?" He nodded towards an empty booth. After we had sat down, he asked, "So, James, what's this all about?"

"I was wondering what you could tell me about a place called the Temple of Transcendental Enlightenment."

Shorty has been a reporter most of his life, either in San Francisco or across the bay in Oakland. He mostly did crime, but he covered politics and business, too, if the need arose. As a kind of sideline, he had become a student of the quirky side of the city. He knew as much about the city's charlatans, cults, and nut jobs as anyone.

"What's the interest?"

"I trailed a suspect there tonight. I'd like to have an idea of what he was doing there."

Shorty paused for a moment, drawing himself up as if getting ready to make a speech.

"I'll tell you what I know, James, but it isn't that much. The bunch associated with the Temple are a secretive lot. What I do know is that the place is run by a character that goes by the name of Aleister Conklin. Whether that is his real name or not, I haven't a clue. He claims to be British, and for all I know, that might even be true. In any case, he affects an exaggerated sort of accent. Almost theatrical. I do know that he was definitely in England before he came here to San Francisco three or four months ago."

"So you think he's some kind of religious con-man?"

"I didn't say that, James. At least not in the usual sense. As far as I know, the Temple doesn't go in for the usual business of fleecing little old ladies out of their pension money. There's money involved of course, but it seems to be coming from people with more cash than sense.

"Conklin claims to be some sort of magician. Not the stage sort, mind you, but the real thing, or at least that's what he says. He wrote a book back about fifteen years ago. There was a lot of stuff in it about invoking the dark powers, channeling demons, and that sort of nonsense. All pure rubbish, of course, but it seemed to have attracted to him a small but loyal following, both here and in England."

"I see," I commented, thought I didn't really.

"He seems to prey on the rich and feckless, the younger sons and daughters of money out looking for a thrill. There have been allegations of drug use and sex orgies, but then that's no different than Hollywood these days, is it? I'm not sure how much stock to put in them, but it might explain how he keeps his followers loyal.

"Conklin claims to be heir to all sorts of ancient mystic lore. That's not so unusual in these cases, but he appears to have taken it further than most. He seems to have become fixated on the idea of achieving immortality, the real kind, not the literary. There are rumors, unsubstantiated, mind you, that he actually has engaged in some dark rituals, possibly including human sacrifice, towards that end. If so, I gather that it went badly, and that was the reason he had to leave England rather hurriedly."

"Sounds like a nice chap," I quipped.

"Don't take him too lightly, James. From what I hear, Conklin isn't afraid to play rough if need be, and some of his associates are pretty nasty types. Take the combination of crazed drug fiends and dreams of immortality and you have all the makings of a new religion. There are too many fanatics in this world as it is. Any of this any help?"

"I'm not sure, Shorty. It seems kind of a stretch—"

"What's your angle on this, James? I've spilled my brains for you; you owe me something. I am, after all, a newspaperman."

"I can't tell you too much right now, Shorty, but, if things develop I'll let you have the inside scoop."

"At least tell me what case you're working on."

"I'm not at liberty to tell you who I'm working for, but I'm trying to find a book."

A sly look crossed Shorty's face as he peered into his glass. "Does this have anything to do with the Levi murder, James?"

"How did you hear about that?" I asked, surprised.

Shorty looked offended. "I'm a crime reporter, James. I read the police reports. They mention that a rare manuscript was stolen from Levi's shop. I presume that's the book you are looking for?"

"Like I said, Shorty, I can't answer that, but I will tell you that I'm not working for the public library."

"Have it your way, James. But what's the connection with the Temple? Do you think Conklin killed Levi and stole the book?"

I took a drink of whiskey before answering. "There may not be a connection, Shorty. It's just that I was following someone close to the book and he went into the Temple. Maybe he was just looking for some transcendental enlightenment, but he doesn't strike me as the type. Of course, I could be wrong. I don't know him very well."

Shorty, who had been doing most of the talking had fallen behind on his drinking, took time to make up on it. When he put the glass down he looked me in the eye and said, "Watch your back, James. And don't underestimate Conklin just because he sounds crazy. Those can be the most dangerous sort."

"I won't, Shorty," I said getting up.

"And don't forget to let me know if anything juicy happens."

I gave him a wave and left.

CHAPTER 9

The next day I spent the first half hour at my office reading the morning papers. I mostly skip the international news and sports, but in my line of work I find keeping up on the local news can be very useful. I was particularly interested in what was being said about the Levi murder, which wasn't much. Mostly it was the usual bunk about how the police were "completely baffled." I thought Lt. Miller would appreciate that.

One item in the society column caught my eye. It stated that a well known east coast millionaire was staying in town for a few days after returning from an extended trip to the Orient. While in town he would be staying at the Hotel Alexandria and was expected to attend several social functions during his stay. All of this would have been irrelevant except for one small detail; the millionaire was one of the names on the list that Miss Lanier had sent me.

Now it occurred to me that it just might be a coincidence. People with plenty of money do travel a lot, and chances were that lots of people returning from the Orient would pass through San Francisco. You won't find many detectives, though, that believe in coincidences. Besides, I didn't have a lot of leads to follow. If nothing else, it was worth checking out.

The Hotel Alexandria isn't far from my office, just a few blocks up Sutter in the direction of Union Square. Being that close, there was no point in wasting cab fare. Ten minutes later I was standing in the lobby trying to spot the hotel detective.

I won't say that Gene McCarthy is a friend of mine, but I try to keep on good terms with him. He's an ex-cop from the other side of the bay who got on the wrong side of a police captain who didn't like Irishmen. Being a hotel dick doesn't pay much, but it's inside work, and, if you know the right angles, you can do okay for yourself. McCarthy had been around long enough that he knew the angles.

McCarthy saw me before I found him. He looks older than his age, with blood-shot eyes and legs stiff from stranding around for too many hours on marble floors. Passing me by, he caught my eye and nodded towards an out of the way corner of the lobby. I waited a moment and then headed in that direction.

I'd picked up a pint of rye on the way to the hotel, and palmed it when we shook hands. McCarthy didn't bat an eye, and the pint disappeared into the pocket of his suit coat.

"What are you up to, Jim?" McCarthy asked, as if nothing had passed between us and he was just doing his job.

"Just sight-seeing, Gene. I was reading the society column this morning and heard you had a genuine millionaire staying here. I thought I might get a glimpse of him."

"Not likely. He's staying up in the top floor suite and hasn't come out since he arrived. Kind of out of your league, though, isn't he? No offense meant."

"None taken. I'm not so much interested in your guest as in anyone that might come to visit him."

This got a raised eyebrow from McCarthy.

"What's up, Jim? I can't let you go bothering our guests, at least ones with that much loot."

"I'm trying to find an item that was stolen."

"You can't think that our guest would be involved in something like that. He's got enough money that he can buy anything he wants."

"I'm not suggesting that he stole the item, Gene. It's just that at one time he had expressed interest in buying it. I thought it possible that he might still be in the market. It's whoever is trying to sell it that I'm interested in."

"I wouldn't know about anything like that," McCarthy commented. I could see that he was in a quandary, he didn't want to kill the goose that laid the golden pint, but he didn't want to lose his job, either.

"It's like this, Gene. Whoever stole this item killed a man to get it. The police might be interested—"

"Geez, Jim. Don't go bringing the cops into this. I'll lose my job for sure."

"I wouldn't want you to get into any trouble over this, Gene," I assured him. "That's why I'd like to handle the matter quietly. You let me know if anyone suspicious goes up to see the man on the top floor and I'll try to keep you, the hotel, and him out of it."

"Sure thing, Jim. That'd be grand of you."

"I'm glad we're in agreement, then. There hasn't been anyone out of what you'd expect up to see him already, has there? I'm particularly interested in someone in particular." I described Edward Fenchurch to him.

"No. I haven't seen anyone like that hanging around. But I'll be sure to keep my eyes open."

"Thanks, Gene."

"Say, what is this item, anyway?"

I thought it over and decided there wasn't any harm in telling him. "It's a book. About yay by yay by yay." I illustrated the dimensions of the codex with my hands.

"Look, Jim, if you don't want to tell me, that's your business, but don't lie to me."

"I'm telling you the truth, Gene. It's a book, a very old and rare book, and valuable enough that one man's given his life for it already. You might have read about it, the old Jew that was killed in his shop south of Market."

"Yeah, I read about that. The papers didn't say that something had been taken, though."

"The police are keeping it quiet for the time being. Look, help me on this Gene, and there might be a reward in it for you, and I'm not talking about just another pint of hooch."

McCarthy looked at me appraisingly. "I'll keep my eyes open, Jim."

"Great. I'll be in touch."

As I walked out of the hotel, I was less confident that anything would come of the man staying on the top floor of the Hotel Alexandria. His arrival in San Francisco had almost been too fortuitous to be anything other than a coincidence. As I headed back to my office I tried to figure out what to do next.

There was a message waiting for me at the switchboard in the lobby when I got back to the office. It was from Miss Lanier asking me to call her.

Jeeves must have recognized my voice when I rang her back, because before I had a chance to say anything he said, "If you'll wait a moment, Mr. Tolliver, I'll inform Miss Lanier that you are on the line."

A few moments later a warm voice said, "It's so good of you to return my call so promptly, Mr. Tolliver." I thought that a man could get used to a voice like that.

"No problem, Miss Lanier. I was just out of the office for a moment. Working on the case. I was running down a lead."

"That's what I called about, Mr. Tolliver. Have you made any progress?"

"Some. I haven't had much time—"

"I didn't mean that as a criticism, Mr. Tolliver. Perhaps we could discuss where things stand."

I was used to clients wanting to know where their money was going, so it didn't bother me. "Do you want to go over things now over the phone?"

"I'd prefer to discuss them face to face. I've always found that that leads to fewer misunderstandings."

"I could drop by the house later this afternoon, then, if you'd like, Miss Lanier."

"I'd rather not disturb Mr. Brockington. Perhaps we could meet at your office?"

"If you'd like. It's at 114 Sutter St., room 401. I can be there any time you'd like."

"Would three o'clock be convenient?"

"That would be fine, Miss Lanier. I'll be looking forward to seeing you."

"Good-bye, then. Until three." There was a click as she hung up.

I was left wondering what that little exchange had been about. Was she really concerned about disturbing her employer? I would have thought that that old house would have offered plenty of places where we could talk privately. Or did she want to keep our discussion secret from someone at the house? Someone like Edward Fenchurch, perhaps? Did Miss Lanier have suspicions of her own about the secretary? I had a feeling I'd be finding out.

I was still pondering this when there was a knock at the door. Without waiting for an answer the door opened to reveal Lt. Miller.

"Have you eaten lunch, yet?" he asked without preamble.

I looked at the clock. "It's only eleven, lieutenant."

"Well, I've been working since six this morning, and I'm hungry. I could do with a beer, too. Let's go to lunch."

There didn't seem to be any point in refusing him.

Chapter 10

I was surprised by Miller's invitation. We weren't all that close. Also, unlike a lot of cops I knew, Miller didn't usually drink on duty, especially in the middle of the day. Not that he'd turn down a free beer. He obviously had something that he wanted to get off his chest. I had no scruples about drinking at that hour, and I wanted to hear what was on the lieutenant's mind, so I agreed. I grabbed my overcoat off the coat rack and followed Miller out the door.

There was a bar nearby that served decent sandwiches. If the bartender liked you he'd throw in some potato salad or a cup of soup. It wasn't fancy fare, but it was filling, and at eleven o'clock the place was still quiet and empty. The bartender checked us out as we entered, decided we were okay, and nodded. We didn't bother with one of the few tables, instead grabbing a couple of stools at one end of the bar. There was a guy that looked like a door-to-door salesman at the other end, but he seemed harmless.

After the bartender took our orders and had placed a couple of schooners of beer on the bar in front of us, I asked, "So what's this about?"

"What do you mean?" Miller replied.

"Look, we get along alright, but we aren't in the habit of lunching together. You want something."

Miller looked for a moment as if he was going to deny it, but then gave it up. "It's like this. The captain is on me about this Levi murder. The chief is on the captain because someone in City Hall is on him. Whoever is behind it, they want the case solved and they pull enough weight for it to mean something. The problem is that I've got nothing. No witnesses, no clues, no suspects. About all I know is that Levi was shot in the head from behind and that an old book was taken. I was hoping you had come up with something. I know you're more interested in the book than the old man's killer, but you said yourself, find the book and you've found the killer, find the killer and you've found the book. I was told to cooperate with you. I was hoping that would work both ways."

"Suits me," I responded as the bartender set our sandwiches down on the bar. Mine was corned-beef, Miller had ordered ham and Swiss cheese. Both were on a decent looking sourdough. The bartender must have liked us because there was a scoop of potato salad and a pickle on each plate. "Okay. You tell me yours, I'll tell you mine."

"Like I said, I've pretty much got nothing. There weren't any witnesses, which given the time of death isn't all that surprising. The only prints in the office were Levi's and some of those were weeks old. One of the bright boys compared the books to the money in the cash drawer. As far as he could tell, they matched. You've been in the place. It's impossible to tell if anything was disturbed or taken other than that book of yours."

"I think that was all they were interested in, and I think they were amateurs. If the killer had wanted us to think it was an ordinary robbery, they would have taken the money out of the cash box, but they didn't."

"Yeah. You're probably right. Say, you don't think that this business is some kind of insurance scam, do you? I mean, we only have Brockington's word for it that Levi actually had the book in the first place. Maybe Levi was killed to make it look like he had it so Brockington could collect on the insurance."

"Brockington never mentioned anything about the codex being insured. Besides, insurance companies won't normally write a policy on something like that without the item being appraised. That couldn't have happened until after Brockington had taken delivery on the book. Besides, I got the impression that he wanted to keep the fact that he had the book a secret."

"Right, dumb idea," Miller said, shaking his head.

"What about the murder weapon?" I asked after an awkward silence.

"The doc recovered a slug from the body. It was a .25. They went back to the scene and a shell casing that matched was found that had rolled behind a pile of books. That pretty much proves that the weapon was a .25 automatic pistol. Not that that does us much good. Probably thousands of them floating around this town. We might be able to match the bullet to the pistol if we had the pistol, but the killer was inconsiderate enough to take it with them. That's it for me."

As if to punctuate his statement, the lieutenant took a big bite out of his sandwich, chewing it aggressively. After he had swallowed he said, "Your turn."

"I've been working at it from the other end, trying to figure out how one gets rid of something like that. I asked someone I know, not someone that deals in stolen goods, mind you, but who knows some people that do. His opinion was in line with what we thought earlier, that there's no one local who would deal in anything like the codex. We're probably looking at someone from out east, maybe even Europe."

"So?"

"I got to thinking that maybe the person behind the robbery was one of the people who had bid against Brockington when the codex went up for auction. I asked Miss Lanier if she could come up with a list of the bidders."

"This Miss Lanier, is she a looker?" Miller asked. The lieutenant is happily married with a couple of kids and a fat wife who can cook. That doesn't stop his imagination.

"Not bad, if your ideal is the school marm type. She wears glasses and sensible shoes," I replied.

"The question is, is she your type?"

"Not me. I have a feeling that Miss Lanier is sharper than both of us and knows it. Anyway, I took the liberty of making a copy of the list." I reached into my inside coat pocket and pulled out a folded piece of paper. Miller flattened it out on the top of the bar and looked it over.

"Miss Lanier said that these are only the ones that she knows of. Some of the bidders were using agents and kept their identities secret. I gather that's fairly common with these kinds of things. I figure that you might have better luck than me finding out if any of the people on the list are in town."

"Say, the American on the list, that isn't the same guy that was in the paper, is it?"

"Yeah. He just arrived from the Orient, and he's staying at the Hotel Alexandria. I've had a word with the house dick there and he's going to keep an eye on things."

"You think he's behind the murder? If he is, the chief isn't going to be happy. Arresting millionaires is never fun, not after their lawyers get into the act."

"I don't know. His being in town may just be a coincidence—"

"But you don't think so, do you?" Miller asked.

"I just don't know. That's why I've got the house dick watching him."

"Any other suspects?"

"Nothing solid. I've got a funny feeling about Brockington's secretary, Edward Fenchurch, but that might just be because I don't like him."

"Why him?"

"This whole business has the feel of an inside job. Not many people knew that the book was in town and at Levi's. Fenchurch was one of them. So far, though, that's all I've got on him. That, and like I said, I don't like him. There is one queer thing, though—"

"What's that?" Miller asked, interested.

"I followed him last night, just on account of. I trailed him to a place called the Temple of Transcendental Enlightenment."

"Never heard of it," Miller shrugged.

"I gather that it's fairly new. It's run by a joker named Aleister Conklin. A Brit, or at least he acts like one. I gather it's some sort of mystical mumbo-jumbo demon worshipping cult."

"Sounds like something for the Bunko Squad rather than Homicide."

"I don't think it's a con, or at least not one of the five and dime sort that cheats old ladies out of their pension checks. Conklin seems to have suckered in some youngsters with more money than brains as his followers. Of course, it's possible that Conklin actually believes in his line of hokum."

"So what's the connection between him and this Fenchurch?"

"That's what I'd like to know. Fenchurch doesn't strike me as the kind to go in for the occult stuff, but I could always be wrong. All I know is that he went inside this temple place last night and came out a half hour later.

Conklin isn't one of the names on Miss Lanier's list, but like I said, she didn't know the identity of all the bidders."

"Does this Conklin have that kind of money?"

"If he doesn't, some of his followers probably do."

I finished my sandwich and slid the plate away from me.

Miller, watching, asked "You going to eat that pickle?" When I shook my head he grabbed it. "You got anything else?"

"You got my pickle, what more do you want?"

"I mean about the case," Miller responded defensively.

"No," I admitted. "Oh, there was one other thing. It turns out I'm not the only one looking for the book. There was someone got up as a Catholic priest that was following me yesterday."

"A priest?" Miller said incredulously.

"Yeah."

"Was he legit?"

"After I turned the tables on him, we went up to my office to talk. He showed me some credentials that certainly looked impressive. They said that he was Father Ignatius Donnelly and that he was a representative of the Curia in Rome."

"I wouldn't know about that kind of thing," Miller said. "I'm a Lutheran." Miller comes from someplace in the Midwest and pronounced the "th" in Lutheran as a "t."

"Maybe he really is a priest, but the funny thing is that he was carrying a Luger under his cassock. When I asked him about it he gave me a spiel about being an Irishman caught up in the troubles over there before turning to religion. Seems that now he's some sort of secret agent for the Vatican."

"So what's the Catholic Church want with the book?"

"Donnelly claimed that it originally belonged to the Vatican Library before one of the Borgias checked it out and forgot to return it."

"Sounds like a lot of hooey," Miller commented.

"Hard to say," I responded. "I suppose you could check with the Archbishop, but either way, he'd probably deny knowing anything about the good father. I have a feeling that Father Donnelly's methods aren't exactly orthodox."

"So we got the Catholic Church, a millionaire, and maybe this crazy Conklin guy interested in the book. Anyone else?"

"Whoever stole it, unless that's one of three you named. Except, if any of them stole it, they wouldn't be looking for it, would they?"

"No, I guess not," Miller conceded. He drained the last of his beer, looked longingly at the empty glass, and then thought better of it. As he got up he said, "I've got to get back to work. Let me know if you find anything out."

It was only after he'd left, that I realized that Miller had left me with the tab.

CHAPTER 11

Miss Lanier was punctual, but then I had expected nothing less from her. Precisely at three o'clock there sounded the discrete tap of dainty knuckles on the frosted glass of the outer door to the office. For a moment I speculated whether she had been outside in the corridor staring at her watch waiting for the hour of our appointment, but I realized that would have been much too haphazard for Miss Lanier.

I rose and went to open the door. Instead of the prim schoolmistress of our first encounter, I was greeted by someone much more stylish. The brunette hair had been unleashed from its bun to cascade in a wave down onto her shoulders. Her suit of grey silk had been tailored to accentuate rather than conceal the curves of her body, and the collar of the ivory blouse she wore underneath was parted to reveal the pale lines of her throat. The calves where still shapely, but the sensible shoes had been replaced by high-heeled pumps. Her makeup had been applied so artfully as to be almost invisible. I had to wonder whether she had dolled herself up just for me, or whether the schoolmarm outfit was an act that she reserved for Brockington.

"Please, Miss Lanier, come in and have a seat." I motioned with my hand towards the better of the two chairs facing my desk. I had taken the precaution of dusting the office in anticipation of my guest.

"Thank you, Mr. Tolliver."

She sat down in one long, smooth motion, neither perching on the front edge of the chair, or lounging against the back. Instead, she sat with a perfect posture that accentuated her attributes. As I took my place opposite to her it was difficult not to be distracted by her—attributes.

"May I offer you a cigarette?" I asked, proffering a silver cigarette box.

"No, thank you, Mr. Tolliver. I don't smoke."

I shut the lid of the box and placed it back on the desk. I knew better than to offer her a snort from the bottle of rye I kept in the desk.

"Let's get down to business, Mr. Tolliver. I'd like to know what progress you've made in recovering the codex. As you can imagine, Mr. Brockington is most anxious."

"Very well, Miss Lanier. It's pretty obvious that the object of the robbery was to obtain the codex. Nothing else was taken, not even cash from the safe where the book was kept. It's also clear that Levi knew the killer well enough to let him into his shop after hours. The murder itself was committed with a small caliber automatic pistol, a weapon that could be easily concealed in a man's pocket—or a woman's purse. The police and I are in agreement on these points."

"Are you implying that the killer was a woman, Mr. Tolliver?" she asked sounding more curious than alarmed.

"I'm not implying anything, Miss Lanier. I'm just mentioning possibilities. It seems probable that the robbery was what is called an 'inside job.' The killer knew that the codex had arrived and that it was in Levi's shop. They were also someone who was familiar to Levi. I'd like to ask you, Miss Lanier, just who knew about the arrival of the codex?"

Miss Lanier looked at me from under her long lashes. It didn't strike me as the look of someone that was worried about discovery, but she also struck me as a woman who was in control of her emotions.

"Well, there was Mr. Brockington, of course. Mr. Levi telephoned him upon the arrival of the package. The courier had delivered it around six that evening, and he called just as we were preparing to sit down for dinner. I knew, because Mr. Brockington informed me of the fact, as he did Mr. Fenchurch. There was no one else at dinner and no one else in the house except the staff."

"What about the butler?" I asked, feeling a little silly,

"The butler, Mr. Tolliver?" she replied, sounding confused.

"Did he answer the phone?" I insisted.

"Yes."

"And he knew that the caller was Levi?"

"Well, yes. I remember that he said something like, 'Mr. Levi is on the telephone, sir' when he announced the call."

"Did the butler know anything about the codex?"

"Surely, Mr. Tolliver, you can't think that the butler had anything to do with the crime. Stanley has been with Mr. Brockington for a dozen or more years."

"Oh, I'm not accusing the butler of anything. That kind of thing usually only happens in detective novels. But I am trying to be thorough. Is it possible that the butler had overheard something about the codex and knew that its arrival was anticipated?"

"I suppose it is possible. Mr. Brockington was always discrete in discussing the arrangements for the codex, but you know how it is with servants. They can be invisible at times."

"Would Levi have known the butler?"

"Well, Stanley had, on several occasions, picked up items from the shop that Mr. Brockington had purchased."

"Do you know if the butler left the house that evening?"

"I can't answer that, Mr. Tolliver. Because of his physical condition, Mr. Brockington goes to bed early. I went up to my room around nine, and stayed there until morning. Stanley is responsible for locking up the house, but I couldn't say whether or not he left at some point in the evening."

"So it is possible that the butler knew that the codex was valuable, that it had arrived, and that Levi might have let him into his shop?"

"When you put it that way, Mr. Tolliver, yes, I would have to say that it is possible," Miss Lanier agreed reluctantly. "But I still can't believe that Stanley could have committed murder."

"Oh, I'm not saying that he did. But I do have to consider him a suspect, Miss Lanier. Say, do we have to keep going on with this 'Miss Lanier' and 'Mr. Tolliver?' I know it's polite and proper, but it just seems to get in the way of our conversation."

She seemed amused by the suggestion. "Just what do you propose—Mr. Tolliver?"

"Just that we be a little less formal. You can call me Jim if you'd like or James."

"I see. And I suppose that you would like to call me Gail?"

"Something like that. It does seem better than Abigail."

"Very well—James."

"Good. About this butler, Stanley. Is that his first or last name, Gail?"

"You know I'm not sure," she answered, momentarily puzzled.

"Could you find out for me? I'd like to check up on him. Just to be thorough."

"Of course. Have you discovered anything else?"

"You don't just steal something like the codex on speculation; you have to have a buyer in mind beforehand. I've discussed the matter with—well, local sources, let's say, and there doesn't seem to anyone in San Francisco either as a thief or a receiver of stolen goods that would deal in anything like the codex. That means that we're probably looking at someone from out of town as the buyer. That's why I was interested in that list you gave me."

"I see. And was it of any use, James?"

"It may just be a coincidence, but one of the names on that list, the American, just arrived in town from the Orient."

"Yes. I saw that in the newspaper. You don't think he had anything to do with this business, do you? He's so respectable."

It's funny how so many people equate rich and respectable. Usually, I've found just the opposite to be true.

"I've made some discrete inquiries in that direction, but so far nothing indicating his involvement has turned up."

"I'm glad to hear that, James. He comes from such an old family."

"Speaking of old, I did find one other party that seems to be interested in the codex."

"Who would that be?"

"The Catholic Church. There's a man named Ignatius Donnelly. He claims that he's a priest working for the Vatican. He showed me papers to prove it, but there was something not quite kosher about him, like the fact that he was packing a Luger pistol."

"That does seem odd behavior for a priest, James."

"Yeah, I thought so. Anyway, he claims that the book was checked out of the Vatican Library by one of the Borgias and never returned. It seems they want it back, the Vatican

I mean, not the Borgias. The question is, how far is this Father Donnelly willing to go to repossess it?"

"I'm an Episcopalian, myself, but I would like to think that even a Catholic priest wouldn't resort to murder."

"You wouldn't think so. I believe there's even a commandment about it. What do you think, though, about the church having a claim on the book."

"The Codex has had a long and checkered history, James. It's had many owners and exchanged hands many times, not always through legitimate means. Who's to say if the church's claim is valid. I do know that Mr. Brockington paid a great deal of money to obtain the Codex."

"And as long as he's paying the bills, I'll go along with that. There is one other thing--"

"What's that?"

"Just how well do you know Fenchurch?"

"Edward?" The way she said the name led me to think that they were on familiar terms, but not close.

"I'm not asking anything personal, Gail. I mean his background, his character, things like that?"

"Not much, really. I mean we work together, but we aren't really confidants. I do know that he was educated at some Midwestern school, Northwestern, I believe. He seems to be good at his job. At least he keeps Mr. Brockington satisfied. But other than that—"

"You wouldn't happen to know if he is into the occult or anything like that, would you?"

"Edward?" she said with surprise. "I wouldn't think so. I wouldn't think he'd have the imagination for that. That's a curious question. Why do you ask?"

"Last night I followed him to a place called the Temple of Transcendental Enlightenment. It's run by a man named Aleister Conklin who fancies himself some sort of wizard or magician or something like that. I thought the visit—well, odd."

"I can't imagine what Edward would be doing in a place like that, James. You said that you were following him. Does that mean that you are following me as well?"

"I haven't, as yet, Gail. That doesn't mean that I won't. I can think of plenty of less pleasant people to tail."

"I don't know when to take you seriously, James."

"Sometimes I don't know, myself. Getting back to Fenchurch, you wouldn't happen to know if he had a pistol? A small one?"

"He's never mentioned one to me. As far as I know, I wouldn't think that he's ever shot a gun in his life."

"Does Brockington keep any guns in the house?"

"There are a couple of hunting rifles in the study."

"Nothing smaller?"

"Not that I'm aware of."

"Just checking details. That's mostly what detectives do, you know."

"It must be an odd profession, James. Sometime you'll have to tell me more about it." It wasn't quite an invitation, but it was close.

"I'd like that, Gail. Is there anything else you'd like to know?"

"Not unless you have something more that's relevant to the codex."

I shook my head.

"I'd better be going then, James. I still have some errands to run for Mr. Brockington before I go back to the house."

It wasn't a brush off, but I could tell that the meeting was over. I escorted her to the door and then watched her walk down the corridor to the elevator. It was quite a sight.

CHAPTER 12

My conversation with Miss Lanier had been pleasant but not particularly enlightening. I didn't really think of the butler as a likely suspect, though I would have to check out his past, or rather have Lt. Miller do it. He had access to resources that could handle that job far better than I could.

By the process of elimination, Edward Fenchurch kept bubbling up to the top of the heap as the leading suspect. He had known about the arrival of the codex and presumably had been known well enough by Levi that the latter would have let him in. Whether he had the contacts to dispose of the codex was still to be established, but that was at least plausible.

My only contact with Brockington's secretary to that point had been a brief conversation over the phone and the few moments in the study before the arrival of his boss. I needed to remedy that situation, and now seemed like the perfect opportunity, especially as Miss Lanier would still be occupied running errands.

To save time, I took a cab over to Brockington's house. If Stanley, the butler, was surprised at my presence when he answered the door, he didn't show it, but then, I suppose that's all part of being a butler.

"I'm sorry, Mr. Tolliver, but Miss Lanier isn't home," the butler said after allowing me into the entry hall.

I thought about asking him whether Stanley was his first or last name, but decided against it. If he was to be a suspect, I didn't want to tip my hand.

"That's all right. Actually, I wanted to speak with Mr. Fenchurch if he's at home."

"I'll see if he's available. If you'll wait here, sir." He took my hat and coat and disappeared.

I cooled my heels for a couple of minutes before Fenchurch appeared. He was dressed impeccably in a lounge suit and an ascot. Every one of his thinning hairs was in place. For that alone, I wanted him to be guilty of stealing the codex.

"Stanley said that you wanted to speak with me—" His manner was cool but polite.

"I've got a few questions for you, if you don't mind. Routine, you understand, but still something I need to do."

"Of course. Perhaps it would be better if we spoke in my office."

"That suits me."

His office was just off the library. It was a small, but pleasant enough room with a large window looking out onto the street. There was a large desk covered in papers in the middle of it sitting on a Persian carpet. A comfortable chair faced the desk. A bookcase was built into one wall, and several wooden filing cabinets took up much of the wall opposite. I noted that the papers on the desk were all aligned in neat piles.

"Please have a seat," Fenchurch said as he motioned to the chair in front of the desk. He took his place behind the desk where he was framed by the window behind him.

"If you don't mind my asking, just what is it you do for Mr. Brockington?"

For a moment I thought he wasn't going to answer, but then he said, "Mostly, I deal with Mr. Brockington's correspondence and the financial aspects of his collection. His bank and lawyers handle his business interests; I don't have much to do with that, but his purchases of books and manuscripts are handled by me. I also manage the household accounts, but that doesn't involve much. The housekeeper and cook are both quite competent and have worked for Mr. Brockington for some time. I'm not sure, though, how this is relevant to the matter of the codex."

"I'm just trying to get the lay of the land, as it were, Mr. Fenchurch. You see, I've come to the conclusion that the theft of the codex and the murder of Mr. Levi were not random crimes. The killer knew what he was looking for and knew that that codex had arrived at Levi's shop. The implication is that the crime was committed by someone intimate with the household."

I watched Fenchurch closely as I said this, but he didn't react.

"I'm not sure that I agree, Mr. Tolliver. It would seem to me that it is more likely that it was misstep on the part of either Mr. Levi or the courier that tipped off the criminal. That is the correct parlance, is it not, 'tipped off'?"

"It is. At least in the movies," I assured him. "Unfortunately, interviewing Mr. Levi isn't possible. However, it doesn't strike me that he was a careless man."

"He let the thief in, didn't he?" Fenchurch countered.

"Which makes me think that the killer was someone he both knew and trusted."

"There is that," Fenchurch conceded. "What about Mr. Levi's friends or associates?"

"The police are checking on that, and frankly they have more resources than I do in that direction, but it doesn't appear that Levi had many close acquaintances. But you mentioned the courier. Did you make the arrangements for that?"

"No. actually that was handled by Miss Lanier. She was on the scene, you see.   But it was a firm that Mr. Brockington has used before, and they have impeccable credentials. They are used by some of the best museums in the world and many well known dealers in art, both here and abroad."

"I see.   And you say Miss Lanier made the arrangements—"

"Yes. She was coming through London, anyway, on her way home from the auction, and given the value and nature of the codex, it was felt best to deal with the owner of the courier service in person. Say, you aren't implying that Miss Lanier had anything to do with the theft, are you?"

I thought for a moment that Fenchurch was going to challenge me to a duel to defend her honor. Up till then, I hadn't thought that there was anything going on between the two of them. He didn't seem her type, but then, I've never been very good at figuring out women.

"Don't get upset, Mr. Fenchurch. I'm not implying anything. I'm just trying to get things straight in my mind. I don't have any reason to suspect Miss Lanier. But getting back to this courier, what, exactly, were the arrangements to transport the codex?"

"The courier took possession of the codex in Vienna, in exchange for a cashier's check. Funds had been transferred to the courier firm for that purpose. Once he was in possession, he travelled overland by express train to Calais where he took the boat train to England. There he boarded a ship bound for New York. From New York he took a plane to San Francisco. Each leg of his journey had been timed so that he spent a minimal time lying over. It was all very professional."

"It sounds like it, Mr. Fenchurch. I don't suppose that you know what the courier's plans were after he had delivered the codex to Mr. Levi?"

"I believe that he was going to fly back to New York, immediately. If so, he couldn't have been the thief."

"No, he couldn't have been. That should be something that can be checked. Do you happen to know the courier's name?"

"I believe he was travelling under the name Jonathan Smythe."

"How original."

"Not his real name, of course," Fenchurch commented.

"There seems to have been a lot of secrecy in all these arrangements. Wouldn't it have been safer and easier just to have had the codex delivered here to the house?"

"Mr. Brockington was concerned that there be no connections made between himself and the codex. You see, it has something of an unsavory past and a number of the previous owners have been murdered. Therefore, there was to be no paper trail that could be traced back to him."

"Pretty strange for a book, if you ask me," I responded.

"I suppose it must seem that way to someone of your— background. No offense intended, Mr. Tolliver."

"None taken, Mr. Fenchurch. A detective learns to have a pretty thick skin. One thing puzzles me, though."

"What's that?"

"If Miss Lanier was responsible for making all the arrangements, how is it that you seem to know all the details?"

"For one, I was present when she discussed them with Mr. Brockington. For another, while Miss Lanier made the arrangements, I was the one who wrote the checks."

"Of course. That would explain it."

"I'm glad you understand, Mr, Tolliver," Fenchurch said sarcastically.

"It's interesting, though—"

"What?"

"Despite all the precautions, I know of at least two other parties that were aware of the fact that the codex was in San Francisco."

"Do you, Mr. Tolliver? Might I ask who?"

"One is an American who was one of the bidders in the auction. The other, oddly enough, is a Catholic priest who claims that he's an agent of the Vatican." I wasn't sure about the American at that point, but I didn't see the need to mention that to Fenchurch.

"How odd. You may be correct, Mr. Tolliver. It might have been better if the codex had been handled in a more direct manner. That might have prevented it being stolen and the death of that unfortunate bookseller."

"It's possible," I conceded. "No use crying over spilled milk, though, is there?"

"No, I suppose not. Do you have any other questions? I want to be helpful, but I do have work to do."

"I do have a couple of quick ones."

"Go ahead," Fenchurch said with resignation.

"Where were you the night Levi was killed? No offense, but I have to ask that of everyone involved."

"None taken. I was here at the house all evening. We had dinner. Mr. Brockington went to bed at nine or so. I worked for a few hours, then went to bed myself."

"Can anyone prove that?"

"Until the end of dinner, Miss Lanier and Mr. Brockington. I saw Stanley as he was locking up. But after that, no. I saw no one until the morning. Is that satisfactory?"

"For now."

"Any other questions?"

"Do you own a pistol, Mr. Fenchurch?"

"No. I'm not a violent man, Mr. Tolliver. Is that all?"

"Yes, I think so. No, now that I think about it, do you happen to know the butler's full name?"

"Stanley?" Fenchurch asked in puzzlement. "Why, yes I do. It's Oscar Stanley."

"Thanks. I'll see myself out."

The butler was waiting with my hat and coat in the hallway.

I didn't bother having him call a cab for me. It was only a few blocks down to catch the Hyde St. cable car. I rode that back towards my office, taking the time trying to decide how much of what Fenchurch had told me was the truth and how much wasn't.

CHAPTER 13

As I approached my office building two men fell into step behind me, one to each side, the classic formation for a snatch. The one on the left had a cloth cap pulled low over his eyes which were shielded by tinted glasses. He was a little short of medium height and thin with a build that is described in fiction as wiry. The other one was taller and heavier with a face that wouldn't win any prizes in a beauty contest. Both were dressed in suits bought off the rack, probably several years earlier. Unless I was mistaken the suits were concealing pistols in shoulder holsters.

The big one I recognized as a man named Jackson from my days working for the National Detective Agency. We'd never worked a case together, but I knew he'd gotten a reputation as a tough guy working as a strikebreaker during the union problems at the docks. It had been things like that which had caused me to leave National and open my own agency.

We'd gone maybe six steps in formation when I turned and asked, "What are you boys up to?"

"There's someone who wants to see you, Tolliver," the skinny one said.

"Oh, who's that?"

"You'll find out."

"What happens if I don't want to see this mysterious someone?"

"Look, Tolliver, this is the way it is. We can do this the easy way or the hard way. It doesn't make much difference to us." This was from the bigger of the two. The way he said it made me think that personally he'd prefer the hard way. I admit this exchange of repartee wasn't the most original, but then tough guys like those two aren't usually long on creativity or imagination.

"In that case, let's go. You've piqued my curiosity."

They must have had a car waiting, because one pulled up, a non-descript sedan with four doors. The driver could have been a copy of the other two except that he was a short red-head. The skinny one opened the rear door and slid in. Jackson pushed me in after him and then got in himself so that I was bookended. It was a tight fit. The skinny one patted me down, but as I wasn't carrying, he seemed satisfied.

It wasn't a long ride, just a few blocks down Sutter to the Hotel Alexandria. The driver pulled up to the curb in front. The skinny one got out first, motioned for me to get out. Jackson slid out after. We marched in lock-step through the lobby to the elevators where Jackson pushed the up button. I looked around for McCarthy, but he was conspicuous by his absence.

The elevator boy seemed to know where we were headed, which turned out to be the top floor. There are only two suites on the top floor of the Hotel Alexandria, one to the right and one to the left of the elevators. Jackson didn't bother to knock, and just opened the door to the left-hand suite. The skinny one ushered me inside.

The furnishings of the suite were very modern, Art Deco with plenty of smooth curves and brushed nickel finishes. The furniture was tubular and didn't look particularly comfortable. The room by the door was outfitted as a sitting room with several doors leading off of it, presumably bedrooms. There was a big sofa in white leather and chrome in the center of the room with a glass topped table in front of it. Several chairs in the same style were arranged facing it. A well stocked wet bar was over against the wall.

I recognized the person sitting on the sofa from the papers that morning. It was the East Coast millionaire, the one that had just arrived from the Orient.

"We have matters to discuss, Mr. Tolliver." There hadn't been any introductions. I didn't think that there were going to be any.

"Suits me. Are you sure you want these two sitting in on the discussion?"

The man on the sofa thought about that for a brief moment before saying, "Wait outside."

"Are you sure about that?" Jackson responded.

"I don't think Mr. Tolliver will cause any problems. Will you?"

"Personally, I don't like problems myself," I answered, trying to sound genial.

The man on the sofa nodded and the two National operatives left.

After they left he asked, "Would you like a drink, Mr. Tolliver?"

"Why not?"

The man on the sofa got up and went to the bar. "Scotch and soda?"

"That's fine with me. I'm easy to please."

He poured some whiskey from a decanter into a glass and added soda from a siphon.

"Ice?"

"Sure."

He added a couple of cubes of ice from a bucket to the drink. He tossed a few more into a second glass and added soda from the siphon. I didn't see him pour any booze into it. He walked back to the sofa and handed me the whiskey.

"Have a seat." He gestured to one of the chairs with his hand and then sat in the middle of the sofa. I sat in the chair and took a sip of my drink. It was very good Scotch.

"I understand that you've been interested in who my visitors are." It was a statement not a question.

"I won't deny it."

"Why, Mr. Tolliver? I value my privacy highly."

I thought about giving him a line, but I didn't see any point in it. Either he was interested in the codex or he wasn't. Coming out in the open might tell me which.

"A few days ago a certain item, a book, was stolen. A man was killed in the process. I've been hired to recover the book."

"And what has this to do with me?"

"I was given to understand that you had previously tried to acquire this book but had been outbid by my client."

"And you think that I had something to do with this robbery and murder, Mr. Tolliver?"

"I didn't say that. I thought it possible, that, knowing of your previous interest in the book, the thief might offer to sell it to you. I don't know who the thief is, yet, but I do have several suspects in mind. I was interested if any of them had approached you."

"I assume the book we are talking about is the Rathcael Codex?"

"Yes."

"Until now, Mr. Tolliver, I hadn't been aware that the codex had gone missing. Just who is your client?"

"I'm afraid I can't divulge that. Like you, he values his privacy."

"No matter. I have a pretty good idea who he is."

"I assumed you would."

"I must say that you are very direct, Mr. Tolliver. I like that in a man. It makes things so much easier."

"I don't like to beat around the bush."

"Neither do I, Mr. Tolliver. I assure you that I had nothing to do with the robbery, or the murder. Nor have I been approached by anyone trying to sell me the codex. I hope that you believe that."

"I do. At least until I have evidence to the contrary."

"Then you'll stop poking into my affairs?"

I didn't think I was going to get anywhere with that, particularly now that Jackson and Company were on to me.

"I can't say that if I'm following a suspect and he tries to contact you I'll ignore the fact, but the only thing I'm interested in at the moment is recovering the codex. I don't care what else you are up to."

"Fair enough, Mr. Tolliver. I take it that the codex is still at large?"

"I don't know where it is or who has it, if that's what you mean."

"It is. Tell me, out of curiosity, how much are you getting paid?"

"My daily fee plus expenses, and five thousand dollars if I recover the codex."

"Quite reasonable, and yet far less than the codex is worth. Let me ask you a hypothetical question, Mr. Tolliver. If you were to recover the codex, would you be willing to turn it over to someone other than your client in exchange for, say, ten thousand dollars, to pick a round figure?"

"That's a pretty round figure, but that's not the way I work."

"No, I didn't think it was. Still, keep it in mind, Mr. Tolliver. If you'll excuse me now, I have an engagement I must get ready for. Good day."

I got up and drained the rest of my drink. There was no sense in wasting good booze. Jackson and his pal didn't make any effort to stop me when I left the suite. Riding down in the elevator I thought over the meeting. I was pretty sure the man in the top floor suite hadn't been involved in the theft even if he was still interested in acquiring the codex, which still left me short of suspects.

Down in the lobby I spotted McCarthy. He must have seen me first because he was walking away. I caught up to him and dropped a hand on his shoulder and asked, "What's the big idea?"

"I don't know what you mean, Jim."

"You ratted me out to the man upstairs. That's what I mean."

"Look. I was just doing my job. He's a guest at the hotel. Besides, he paid me fifty bucks to let him know if anyone was nosing around about him. What was I suppose to do?"

I thought about it a moment and laughed. "Nothing, Gene. You did just what I would have done." I slapped him on the back and walked out of the lobby.

I walked the few blocks back to my office. It was early evening. The streetlights had come on and I could feel the cold and the damp coming off the bay I'd had a busy day, but I wasn't all that sure that I had much to show for it.

When I got to my office, I placed a call to Homicide. Somewhat surprisingly, Miller was still working.

"I hope your day has been going better than mine. I'm not having much in the way of luck," Miller said, sounding discouraged.

"A lot of that going around," I replied, commiserating with him.

"So why did you call?"

"I've uncovered a couple of things that might be worth checking out. I thought you might have better luck at it than me."

"So, on top of everything you want me to do your job, is that it?" Miller responded.

"Something like that."

I thought he was going to say something else, something rude, but in the end all he said was, "Okay. What have you got?"

"I just had an interesting conversation with the American on Miss Lanier's list. He sort of invited me up to his suite." I went on to describe the particulars of the meeting.

"You think this millionaire had anything to do with the killing?" Miller asked after I had finished my account of the interview.

"Probably not," I conceded. "But I think it's possible that if the killer's original plans for disposing of the codex fall through he might try to strike a deal with him."

"Maybe I'll set one of my men to watch him just in case. I don't have anything else for them to do."

"It might be worth it," I commented. "I got one other name for you to check up on. His name is Oscar Stanley, and he's Brockington's butler. I'm not sure, but I think he may originally have come from out east someplace, probably New York or Boston."

"So now you think the butler did it?" Miller asked sarcastically.

"There were only a few people that knew that the codex had arrived and what it was worth, and most of them were in Brockington's household. It's possible that the butler did a little eavesdropping. Of course, he's been with Brockington for a dozen years or so, but maybe he's thinking of retiring and the thirty grand the codex is worth would give him a nice nest egg."

"Yeah. I'll make inquiries, as they say. Of course, if he has a crooked past, Oscar Stanley might not be his real name—"

"That thought had occurred to me, but it's all I've got to go on."

"Well, who knows? Something might turn up. I'll let you know if I hear anything."

I said "Thanks" just as I heard the line go dead.

I was tired, hungry, and in need of a drink. I turned out the lights and was locking up in preparation for going home when a black clad form appeared on my doorstep.

CHAPTER 14

"You again," I said to the priest, as I stood with the key in my hand.

"I'm afraid it is, Mr. Tolliver," Father Donnelly said. "I think you and I have a few matters to discuss."

I gave a sigh then said, "You might as well come in, then."

I turned the lights back on and motioned to the chair in front of the desk.

"Have a seat, padre. I don't know about you, but I'm going to have myself a drink."

I pulled the bottle of rye out of the desk drawer along with the pair of glasses. I poured a couple of fingers in one and then cocked an inquiring eye at the priest.

"Bless you, my son, I don't mind if I do. This California weather is enough to chill a man's soul."

"If you wanted warmth, padre, you should have gone to the other end of the state. I hear Los Angeles is pretty nice this time of year."

"Alas, I don't control my own destiny. That's in the hand of God."

I poured some rye in the second glass, shoved it towards him saying, "Well, put that in the hand of man."

The padre said something like "Bless you my son," and took a sip.

"Now, what was it you wanted to discuss, padre?"

"I take it you've not had success in your search?"

"Oh, I've been going through the motions. I've followed a few leads, but I can't say that they've led anywhere."

"That's unfortunate." I noticed that as the whiskey took effect, the padre's Irish brogue deepened.

"Why the interest, padre? If I find the book, I'm just going to turn it over to Brockington. You know that, don't you?"

"Oh, I'm counting on it. You see, if the codex is recovered, at least I will know where it is. Then the church can try to use persuasion, or, failing that, legal means to recover it."

"Good luck with that, padre. Brockington doesn't strike me as the kind of man that will give something up easily. Just why is the Vatican so set on getting this book back? After all, it's been missing for five or six hundred years. I would have thought that the church has enough old things lying around that one more wouldn't be a big deal."

Father Donnelly took a long pull on his glass, savoring the bite of the whiskey as it burned down his throat.

"Just how much do you know about the codex, James? You don't mind if I call you James, do you?"

"James will do fine, padre. I've been called a lot worse."

I was beginning to develop a liking for the priest. At his heart, I sensed that he was one of those legendary Irish rogues, amusing, likeable, but still a rogue for all of that.

"But back to my question. How much do you know about the codex?"

"Not much. I know roughly how big it is. I know it's handwritten in Latin. I know it's old."

"But what do you know of its contents? What the codex is about?"

"Hardly anything. Miss Lanier told me the author was obsessed with sex. I've seen a photo of one of the pages, and that seemed a bit risqué for the church to be interested in it."

"I assure you, James, that the Rathcael Codex is much more than an eleventh century volume of pornography."

"You'll have to enlighten me, padre."

The priest drained his glass and said, "I'm afraid this is going to be a rather long story, James. It might be best if you freshened up our glasses. We have a long evening ahead of us."

I took the padre at his word and poured three fingers into each of the glasses. I eyed the level of whiskey in the bottle and wondered if it would see us through the night.

"Bless you, my son, and forgive me for that which I am about to reveal to you.

"Towards the end of the eleventh century, the third baron of Locksey established a small monastery near the village of Rathcael which is in the west of Ireland some fifty miles southwest of Limerick. As with many Irish monastical establishments, the one at Rathcael had a scriptorium dedicated to the creation of holy texts. There was nothing particularly special about the scriptorium at Rathcael. It employed a handful of monks who produced one or two manuscripts a year, mostly of the usual subject matter, the Gospels, prayer books, etc.

"The patron of the monastery, Brian, third baron of Locksey, was, for his time, an unusually well educated man in that he could both read and write. He was also a man, I won't say of unnatural tastes, but rather of excessive natural tastes. He was obsessed with the sexual act, both in and out of marriage, but mostly without. It is also rumored that he dabbled in black magic, but of course, those rumors come from several centuries later and are probably not altogether accurate. What does seem to be the case is that he was familiar with the druidic lore that was prevalent at

the time. With this background, the baron appears to have developed some rather fantastical theories relating to the—
"

The padre paused at this point as if unsure how to proceed.

"There is no way to put this delicately, James. The baron became obsessed with the notion that the act of sexual congress was a source of mystical power, and that this power could be used for the purpose of obtaining physical immortality. You can understand that the Church, both then and now, considers any such idea as extremely heretical and dangerous."

"I can see how that would be the case," I commented.

The padre continued his story, "The baron, using his position as patron of the monastery, suborned the services of a young man by the name of Brother Padraig, who worked in the scriptorium. The baron commissioned Brother Padraig to produce a manuscript detailing his ideas, dictating to him the contents of what has come to be known as the Rathcael Codex, the manuscript that we both seek for our different reasons. Brother Padraig, it appears, became totally consumed by the project, illuminating the pages with exceedingly graphic depictions of the act of sexual congress from what is to be hoped his active imagination."

I had to smile at the difficulty that Father Donnelly, admittedly, in many ways, a man of the world, had in describing the contents of the codex.

"In due course, after several years, the manuscript was completed and turned over to the baron. Shortly after that event, Brother Padraig met an untimely demise. How he died is not clear. The monastery was plundered and destroyed in the time of Cromwell, and any records it might have held vanished, but it seems probable that Padraig death was unnatural, either suicide or murder.

"The baron's fate was similarly untimely. He married three times, each of his wives dying shortly after their marriage. After the death of the third wife, it appears that the Baron went mad and was confined to a tower of his castle. Shortly thereafter, he either jumped, or was thrown, out of the tower and met his death.

"Upon his death, the abbot of the monastery, who had known of the nature of the codex but been unable to prevent its creation, took possession of the book. Well aware of the unholy nature of the volume, he entrusted it to one of the most trusted brothers of the monastery, who bore it to Rome where it was consigned to the collection of proscribed books in the Vatican Library."

"If the abbot considered the codex was so dangerous, why didn't he just destroy it?"

Donnelly pondered this for a moment. "I suspect that he considered that above his pay grade," the padre answered. "He passed on the responsibility for the fate of the codex to his superiors."

"For the next four hundred years the codex languished in the stacks of the Vatican Library until the latter days of Pope Alexander VI, also known as Rodrigo Borgia, whose attention it came to. He withdrew it from the library, apparently for his personal study. In the turmoil surrounding the death of Alexander VI, the codex vanished."

At this point the padre paused to take a sip of whiskey and catch his breath.

I took the opportunity to interject, "That's some yarn you've spun, padre, though I'm not sure how relevant it is to the problem at hand."

"I've not come to the end of the story yet, James," Donnelly explained. "As I said, after the death of Alexander VI the codex disappeared from Rome. It reappeared at the Hapsburg court in Vienna in 1529. A papal envoy was sent to retrieve the manuscript, but unfortunately he was trapped in Vienna when the Ottoman's besieged the city in that year. During the siege, the envoy was killed, some say murdered, and the codex was lost again.

"Over the next few hundred years there are rumors of the codex surfacing at various times and places in Eastern Europe. It is said to have come into the possession of the famous English mathematician and occultist, John Dee, during the period he spent in Bohemia in the later part of the sixteenth century. Dee was a great collector of books on esoteric subjects, so it would not be surprising if he had become interested in the codex. He is known to have owned a copy of The Book of Soyga, a compendium of spells and incantations, some of which are in code. Some say Dee also possessed the Voynich manuscript, a mystical text written in an unknown script, though that is open to some doubt. When Dee returned to England in 1589, the codex appears to have passed into the hands of Dee's friend, the alchemist Edward Kelley. The codex vanished yet again upon Kelley's arrest by Rudolph II, the Holy Roman Emperor.

"It is perhaps through the association with John Dee, that the reputation of the codex began to grow. What had previously been an obscure Irish manuscript now became something of a holy grail for European occultists. It was supposed to contain the secret of immortality as well as much other magical wisdom. However, no copies of any portion of the contents had ever been made, so the reputation of the codex rested on rumors and hope more than actual knowledge.

"What happened to the codex after Edward Kelly is unknown. Rumors have it popping up on a number of occasions in the Balkans during the seventeenth and eighteenth centuries and even as far south as Constantinople, but always it has just as surely vanished.

During this period a number of occultists and mystics frittered their lives away flitting from one eastern city to another searching for the codex, but as far as is known, none was successful.

"The claim is that finally, in 1897, the codex was added to the private collection of a Hungarian nobleman. While in his possession, no one was allowed to study, or even view, the codex. Since the war, the fortunes of the family of this nobleman have suffered, and it is this manuscript that was offered up in a private auction to a select group of bidders. The auction, itself, was held in utmost secrecy. The bidders or their agents were invited to a castle outside of Budapest where they were allowed to view the codex open to a single page. As you are aware, Timeus Brockington made the successful bid."

"If the codex is so important to the Vatican, why didn't they just outbid Brockington?" I asked. "I would have thought that the church had ample resources to do so."

"For the simple reason that the Vatican wasn't invited to," the priest replied. "The existence of the auction and the results only became known after the fact when one of the unsuccessful bidders revealed the details to someone connected with the Vatican Library. Upon receiving that information, I was dispatched to recover the codex."

"By fair means or foul?"

"By fair means only. The Vatican does not condone murder, James. However, I will admit that the definition of what constitutes 'fair means' is somewhat elastic in the minds of my superiors."

I had to smile at that. I got the impression that while the padre wouldn't murder to obtain the codex, he might not be as scrupulous with the idea of purloining it. The conversation paused for a moment while we each took the opportunity to drink our whiskey.

"Let me ask you this, padre," I said. "You don't believe this business about the codex containing the secret of immortality, do you?"

"James, for all my checkered past, I am a man of God. I believe that there is only one way to achieve immortality, and that is to go to heaven. What the codex contains are merely the delusions of a madman."

"So why is it so important, then, for the church to get back the codex?" I queried.

"You mean in addition to the fact that the codex rightfully belongs to the Church?" Donnelly asked. He continued more heatedly, "The codex is heretical in the extreme. Its very existence serves as a temptation to those with weak minds or souls. That's why it was placed on the list of proscribed works in the first place. It can only lead astray those who would attempt its study. Surely that is obvious to even you, James?"

"I wouldn't know, padre. As far as I'm concerned, the codex is just a book in a language that I can't read and probably couldn't understand even if I could. My only interest in it is the five grand Brockington has promised me if I can get my hands on it."

"And you wouldn't consider turning it over to the Church in that eventuality?"

"I've taken Brockinton's money, and given my word. You wouldn't have me break my promise, would you, padre?"

The priest smiled ruefully. "As a man, I admire your principles, James. I had principles once, before I joined the Church. Now, I only have the word of God."

"You didn't come here tonight just to have a drink and tell a yarn, did you, padre? Why are you really here?"

"I've told you how for centuries the codex was sought by those who call themselves mystics and magicians. There are still some such today in this very city, who follow the same course, who seek the codex because they believe it contains the secret of immortality. I think you would be wise to investigate them in your search."

"Did you have anyone particular in mind, padre?"

"I think you may already be aware of them. I speak, of course, of Aleister Conklin and his followers."

"You think he killed Levi and stole the book?"

"I know he came to San Francisco because he knew that your employer had purchased the codex."

"If you think that this Conklin has the book, why don't you go after it yourself, padre?"

"This is your city, James, not mine. You have resources and connections which I do not. Mostly, though, because I think you might be successful where I would not."

"And because I'd be risking my skin and not yours," I commented.

"There is that, James. If you fail, I'll still be around to make a second attempt."

"At least you're honest about it, padre," I said, raising my glass in salute to the priest.

"I don't know for certain that Conklin has the codex, mind you. I can only say that he's a likely suspect."

"Fair enough, padre."

"And James—"

"Yes?"

"If you do go into that nest of vipers, be careful. Conklin and his followers are dangerous people. I believe they may have killed before, and they certainly will be willing to kill again."

"I'll take that under advisement, padre."

"It's getting late now, James. I should be going. Thank you for the whiskey and companionship on a cold and damp night."

I rose and saw the padre out. As he left, he said, "I'll be praying for you, James." I think he actually meant it.

CHAPTER 15

I woke the next morning with a hangover. The padre and I had polished off most of a fifth of rye while he had been recounting the history of the codex, and while I can't speak for Father Donnelly, I hadn't had anything to eat since my lunch with Miller that day. After a shower and a shave I felt a little better, at least good enough to face another day searching for the codex.

I didn't feel up for making breakfast. Instead I paid a visit to a diner down the block from my apartment. My mood was improved after I had wrapped myself around a couple of eggs over easy that had been deposited on a plate of greasy hash-brown potatoes, improved enough to plot my next move as I lingered over a cup of coffee.

I still thought of Fenchurch as the most likely suspect, but I knew that at the least he had been in contact with Aleister Conklin. Donnelly seemed to have his own suspicions about the cult leader, though he had been somewhat vague as to his reasoning. I was willing to think of Conklin as a murderer, but try as I might, I couldn't quite make things hang together. If Conklin or one of his followers had killed Levi and stolen the codex, what had Fenchurch been doing paying a visit to the temple? Conversely, if Fenchurch had been the culprit, the implication was that Conklin wasn't yet in possession of the codex. That, in turn, meant that Fenchurch had the codex stashed somewhere. Had his visit to Conklin's temple been to arrange the terms of the exchange? Had the exchange already happened?

I had a lot of unanswered questions. Whatever his reasons, it had been pretty clear that the padre had wanted me to check out Conklin and his operation. Maybe there was something he knew that I didn't. Maybe he was just playing a hunch. The reality was that at the moment I didn't have any better line to investigate.

I finished my coffee, leaving a generous tip for the waitress. I went to the garage and hired a car for the day. Having an automobile was proving to be useful. If this case panned out and I recovered the codex, I'd have to consider buying one.

It was just after eleven when I was on Russian Hill parked down the street from the Temple of Transcendental Enlightenment. The movies and murder novels make being a detective seem exciting and glamorous. Often, though, the reality involves sitting in a cold car getting a sore butt from sitting too long while waiting for something that may or may not happen. In this case, I wasn't even sure what it was that I was expecting to occur. By two o'clock, I couldn't have proved that anyone even lived in the house. I was debating whether to call off the surveillance when a car pulled up in front of the temple.

The car was a two seat roadster, new and expensive. The canvas top had been put up against the cold and the fog, so I couldn't see the occupants until they got out. When they did get out, I saw two young men in their mid twenties. Both of them were tall and fit in the way that comes from swimming in a pool and playing tennis rather than doing an honest day's work. They were dressed casually, but well, like feckless playboys in the movies.

They went through the gate in the fence and up to the front door. It looked like they belonged, because they didn't bother to knock. One of them produced a key which he used to open the door, and then they disappeared inside. I wrote down the license number on a business card and waited. And waited.

Three o'clock came and then four. The car was still there and neither of its occupants had come out. I decided that they must be some of Conklin's followers. If that was the case, he had enough muscle behind him to be dangerous.

By five I was getting hungry. It was either time to go home or to take some direct action. I chose the latter. It might not have been the brightest thing to do, but then I've never been accused of being a genius.

I walked up to the door. I couldn't hear anything from inside, but that wasn't surprising; they built them well back when the house had been erected. I could see lights from inside in the transom over the door. There was a door bell button next to the doorknob. I pushed it.

One of the young men from the car answered it. He was bigger than I had thought, six three or four, dressed in grey flannels and a tennis sweater that did nothing to hide the muscles underneath. He was blonde with Nordic features and bloodshot eyes that made him look like a slightly dissipated Viking.

"What do you want?" he asked in a voice that was neither hostile nor friendly. The accent was polished and hard to place, as if it came from somewhere between Boston and Oxford.

"I came in search of enlightenment, transcendental or otherwise."

"The Temple is not a public facility," the blonde said, clearly trying to discourage me.

"In that case, I'd like to talk to Mr. Conklin."

"Master Conklin is a busy man."

"Oh, I think he'll see me. We have matters to discuss."

"About what?"

"Just tell him that we both have an interest in the same book." I knew it was a bluff, but what did I have to lose?

"Wait here." The door was shut in my face. A couple of minutes passed before it opened again. The blonde was there as well as his pal, who was an inch shorter but a couple of inches wider through the shoulders and had close cropped dark hair. "The master will see you. Come this way."

I was ushered down a hall and into a room that had probably been meant as a library or study when the house had originally been built. I doubted that the furnishings had come with the house. Oriental chairs and tables, I thought Chinese, were arranged around the periphery of the room, and embroidered silk banners had been hung from the walls. A large Persian carpet took up most of the floor space. It had been defaced with a five pointed star inscribed within a circle. An ornate character in a script I didn't recognize had been placed at each of the vertices of the star. To add to the illusion of Oriental splendor, a large gong, suitable for summoning palace eunuchs or concubines, hung from a stand next to the pocket doors leading to the hallway. Those were the only doors to the room.

"Wait here," the blonde instructed. As he left, he shut the pocket doors behind him. I heard the click of a lock. A quick examination of the windows which were hidden behind banners revealed effective looking steel bars. I wondered just what the padre had gotten me into. I hadn't bothered to carry a gun, on the theory that doing so tends to lead to shooting. Considering the two young men outside, I'm not sure it would have done me much good. I decided to have a seat in one of the Chinese chairs. It wasn't particularly comfortable.

I'm not sure whether Conklin had been busy or just wanted me to cool my heels to soften me up. Time seemed to drag, though when I checked my watch only fifteen minutes had passed. Finally, I heard the click of the lock and the pocket doors parted. I rose to greet the newcomer.

Given the surroundings, I had half expected Conklin to show up in flowing silk robes or some such costume. Instead, he was wearing an impressively well tailored suit that looked like it probably cost more than the jalopy that I had come in. He was lean rather than thin, and not quite as tall as his two minions. His dark hair was slicked back to hang rather far down his neck. The gray at his temples would have made him look distinguished if the Mephistophelean beard hadn't made him look diabolical.

"My aide said you mentioned a book?" he said. His voice, though not particularly loud, projected in the room like an actor's.

"Yes," I answered, not seeing any point in beating around the bush, "an eleventh century illuminated Irish manuscript, velum with board covers, with a hundred and twenty-eight leaves."

"Let's not mince words. You refer to the Rathcael Codex. Just who are you?"

"My name is James Tolliver." I handed him one of my cards.

"This says that you are a private detective, Mr. Tolliver. What have you to do with the Codex?"

"I've been hired to recover the book. You may not be aware of it, but it's been stolen." Conklin didn't bat an eye at the statement, but then I hadn't expected him to.

He replied, "How fortunate," which I thought odd. "Would you like some tea while we discuss the matter?"

"Tea is fine with me." I'm not much of a tea drinker, but I thought that if it would keep Conklin talking that would be all right with me.

"Siegfried, would you fetch some tea for Mr. Tolliver and me?"

It appeared that Siegfried was the blonde, because he was the one that left the room. The dark haired lad remained.

"Please, Mr. Tolliver, have a seat," Conklin said, indicating one of the Chinese chairs. He had turned on the charm, as if it were a light bulb. I sat. He sat as well in a chair next to mine with an ornately carved table between us.

"I assume, Mr. Tolliver, that seeing as you are here, you have not yet recovered the Codex."

"That would be a reasonable assumption," I agreed cordially.

"What I fail to see is why you have come to me. Do you suspect me of having stolen it?"

I was saved from having to answer that question by the return of Siegfried. They must have already had a kettle on boil because he was carrying a tray with two small cups and a porcelain tea pot. Siegfried set the tray on the table between Conklin and me. Conklin, playing the perfect host, poured from the pot into the two cups.

"Oh, I make it a practice to suspect everyone. That way I'm sure to be right at least once."

"Very amusing, Mr. Tolliver. But I'd really like to know why you would think to suspect me?"

"Your name has come up several times in the course of the case. Nothing definite, of course, but I thought it worth checking out."

"I see," Conklin said. I couldn't tell if he was surprised or not. "Please don't neglect your tea, Mr. Tolliver."

He reached for his cup and sipped daintily from it. Not wanting to cause a fuss, I emulated him. The tea was hot and faintly bitter.

"Out of curiosity, just who is it that has been mentioning my name?"

"Like I said, several people. One was an Irish priest by the name of Donnelly." I saw no need to keep the padre's identity secret. After all, he was the one that had put me in the position I was in.

"I'm unfamiliar with the clergyman," Conklin remarked. "I take it he has an interest in the Codex as well?"

"Yes. He has a notion that the book was checked out of the Vatican Library, and that its return is overdue." I thought that the room was becoming overly warm and wondered if they had turned up the furnace to make me sweat.

"You mentioned several people, Mr. Tolliver—"

I didn't want to mention Fenchurch, but I found myself unable to resist, as if Conklin had worked some hypnotic trick on me.

"My employer's secretary, Edward Fenchurch. I believe he paid you a visit the other night." I didn't know why I said that, but then I wasn't feeling quite myself.

"I assume your employer has said he will reward you if you recover the Codex. Would you be willing to accept counteroffers, Mr. Tolliver?"

"I'm afraid I don't work that way, Mr. Conklin."

"That's really too bad, Mr. Tolliver."

The room began to spin. Then it faded to black.

CHAPTER 16

I woke with a hangover much worse than the one after my night with the padre. I had the chills and the shakes as well. I thought there was something wrong with my eyes, too, but then I realized that was because I was in a place with no light. It was cold and damp, with a dirt floor, as if I was in the cellar of the house. I hoped it was the cellar and not someplace worse.

There appeared to be something wrong with my hands. I found it difficult to move them. Gradually, I realized that was because they were connected by chains to a staple in a rough stone wall. The iron manacles that chafed my wrists felt like they were antiques which didn't make them any less effective. I tried pulling on the chains to see how secure the staple was fixed in the wall, but all that accomplished was to leave me exhausted. I slumped back against the wall to rest.

In hindsight, it was obvious that the tea had been doped. The padre had pointed me at a trap and, like a fool, I'd taken the bait. I wondered if Donnelly was in league with Conklin, though that didn't seem likely. That didn't stop me from wanting to wring the padre's neck.

I must have passed out then from some lingering effect of whatever drug Conklin had added to the tea. When consciousness returned, my muscles were stiff from sitting there in the cold. I tried to stand up, but a wave of nausea came over me. Rolling over on my side, I tried to vomit, but all that happened was a convulsion of my stomach that left me weak from the effort. For a moment I thought I was going to black out again.

While I waited to recover, I realized that the cellar wasn't completely dark. High up on the wall opposite me there was a small window that periodically lit up from the headlamps of a passing automobile. It was cold comfort, but at least it allowed me to confirm that I was chained up in a cellar.

As I sat there, I considered my options. I didn't seem to have many. I thought about shouting for help, but gave that up. Chances were that the only ones that would be able to hear me were my captors. The temple building was a large one and the neighboring houses were set a ways apart. Besides, in the condition I was in, I wasn't sure how loud a noise I could make. The chains that ran from the manacles to the wall were just long enough to allow me to stand, but not much more. Even without the lingering effects of the drug, I wouldn't have stood a chance against Conklin's followers. The only other option I could see was to wait and see what happened. I waited. At least I hadn't been killed outright which left some hope for my continuing survival.

I don't know how long I sat there. There was no way to mark time. I tried counting seconds, but my mind kept wandering, and I'd lose count. I think the drug must have affected my time sense, because it seemed like days had passed before I heard the sound of feet descending a wooden staircase.

Suddenly the cellar was illuminated by a light so dazzling that I had to shut my eyes. After a few moments, I opened them a slit to realize that the light came from a single electric bulb dangling from the ceiling.

Conklin was standing there as well as Siegfried and his pal.

"Good, you are awake, Mr. Tolliver," Conklin said.

"You're mistaken, Conklin. I'm asleep and having a nightmare. I'm sure about that, because this couldn't be happening in real life."

"Still playing the wise cracking detective, Mr. Tolliver? I had thought those only existed in popular fiction."

"Oh, there are a few of us in real life, if that's what this is."

Conklin laughed then, a hollow sound that echoed through the cellar.

"Out of curiosity, what was it that you slipped into my tea?"

"Oh, that? That was just a little something that I discovered in an old book. The ancients had a remarkable pharmacopeia. It's mostly harmless, I assure you, and the effects are temporary. But enough of this banter, Mr. Tolliver. Where is the Codex?"

"I thought we went over that before you slipped me the mickey. I don't know where the codex is. If I did, I wouldn't have come visiting."

"That's unfortunate—for you. It would mean that I would have no reason to keep you alive. Come now, surely you must have some idea where the Codex is or who has it. Help me obtain it, Mr. Tolliver and I might release you from this dungeon. I might even choose to reward you."

"Have you asked Fenchurch? I know he paid a call on you the other night."

"So you know about that, do you?" Conklin asked cocking an eyebrow. "Maybe you are more resourceful than you seem. Just how much do you know?"

"I have this notion that Fenchurch might have been trying to shop the book to you then."

"It was actually the other way around. I had approached Mr. Fenchurch about his willingness to assist me in my quest."

"Was he?" I asked.

"Oh, he was willing enough. Willing enough to discuss terms. However, he said that he wasn't in possession of the Codex, though he had some idea of who was. We discussed terms in a general sort of way and then he departed. I have some doubts, though, as to whether he will be able to deliver."

"Maybe he has other buyers in mind. I know of at least a couple of other parties interested in the book." I admit I was playing for time, though I didn't have any idea of what I expected to do with it. It wasn't as if I was telling Conklin anything that would do him any good.

"You speak of the American?"

"Oh, him, and an agent of the Vatican."

"The Vatican? I'm surprised—and curious. I'd forgotten, but you did mention a priest in our earlier conversation. Tell me more, Mr. Tolliver."

"There's an Irish priest running around town, a Father Donnelly." I didn't feel any particular need to protect the padre's identity. After all, he was the one that had gotten me into the fix I was in.

"A priest you say?"

"Yes. I admit I'm not up on the details of church doctrine, but he struck me as a queer sort of priest. The padre runs around with a Luger where his rosary beads should be. He told me the codex had been checked out of the Vatican Library sometime around 1500 and that he was suppose to get it back. He didn't mention anything about the fine for it being overdue, which is just as well, I guess. After four hundred odd years I expect that would be a doozie."

"Tell me, Mr. Tolliver, do you think this priest, this Father Donnelly, was responsible for stealing the Codex?"

"No, I wouldn't want you to get the wrong impression about the good padre, Conklin. I know he goes around packing a pistol, and I suspect that he knows how to use it, too, but I doubt if he would stoop to murder. He is, after all, a man of God. He might steal, but I don't think he would kill a man in cold blood like that."

"But still, a dangerous player in the game?"

"Oh, that he is. I have a feeling the padre can take care of himself."

"I'll keep that in mind," Conklin said. I was getting the feeling that he was finding our conversation entertaining. He struck me as a bit mad, and madmen crave audiences. From what I'd seen of them, I didn't think that Siegfried and his buddy provided Conklin with much intellectual stimulation. Perhaps he saw me as chance to expound to someone receptive to the strength of his personality. I saw no reason to disabuse him of the idea.

"Tell me, out of curiosity again, just why you want this book so badly? The padre gave me a short synopsis of its history, but I have the impression that he may have left some things out."

"No doubt. Just how much have you been told?"

"Not a lot. The padre said that the manuscript had been commissioned by an Irish nobleman that had some—shall we say—odd ideas about the power of sex. According to him, the codex was meant to be more than just a piece of eleventh century pornography."

"Oh, it's much, much more than that, Mr. Tolliver, I assure you. The Irish nobleman, as you term him, was heir to a thousand years of Druidic lore, secrets that can only be imagined today. The Codex contains nothing less than the secret of immortality." Conklin was getting enthusiastic about the subject.

"The padre hinted at something like that," I said, trying to encourage him.

"Oh, it's more than a hint, Mr. Tolliver. Why else would a man like Rodrigo Borgia have been interested in the Codex? A number of druid mages were reputed to have lived for hundreds, even thousands of years. Take Merlin, for example. He had lived for ages before his association with Arthur."

"I wouldn't know about that. Before my time."

"But it's true, nonetheless. Can you blame me for wanting to possess the Codex?"

"Well, if what you say is true—"

"And it is."

"—I can see the attraction."

"Is it possible that you already have the Codex, Mr. Tolliver?"

"It wouldn't do me much good if I did, Conklin. I don't read Latin."

"Ah, but I do, Mr. Tolliver. Despite your current predicament, you strike me as a man with some useful qualities. My followers, loyal as they are in some respects, are lacking in certain practical aspects. If you were to aid me in my search for the Codex, I would be willing to reward you, Mr. Tolliver, reward you handsomely."

"With what?" I asked, trying to sound like I was giving the idea some serious consideration.

"Why, I would have thought it obvious. With immortality, Mr. Tolliver, eternal life. But that would only be possible if I were to obtain the Codex, of course."

I was beginning to think I might have pushed Conklin over the edge.

"It's an attractive offer, I have to admit. I'd have to think it over, of course. It's not something one commits to casually."

"Of course. Take all the time you like, Mr. Tolliver. In fact, as I have other matters to attend to, I'll leave you to your considerations. Come Siegfried. Let's leave Mr. Tolliver to think it over."

Conklin turned to leave, followed by his minions. A moment later the light bulb went out leaving me in darkness.

Sometime later, I heard a faint scratching. It was coming from the direction of the cellar window. As I looked, it slowly swung open, and a shadowy figure in black squeezed through the opening and lowered itself to the floor.

CHAPTER 17

In the gloom of the cellar, I couldn't recognize the newcomer, but I felt a hint of hope. Whoever had entered my dungeon was clearly not one of Conklin's followers. But was he a potential rescuer or just a burglar set on ransacking the house?

Suddenly a beam of bright light pierced the darkness. The intruder had equipped himself with a small but powerful electric flashlight. Uncertain whether to call out or remain silent, I remained silent as the beam flashed back and forth around the cellar until it finally fell on me.

"Well, boyo, this is a fine mess you seem to have gotten yourself into." Though I couldn't see the face, I recognized the brogue as that belonging to Father Donnelly.

"It seems to me that you're the one that got me into this mess," I replied in a whisper.

"I suppose there's some justice in that," the padre responded. "I must accept at least some of the responsibility."

"We can talk about that later, padre. I'd appreciate it if you could get me out of these." I held up the manacles to see what I meant.

"A bit primitive. Almost medieval. I'm not sure that I'm equipped for something like that. Maybe there's a key around here someplace," the priest said cheerfully. He flashed his light around until it rested on something hanging from a nail in one of the support posts. I noticed that it was just out of reach from where I was chained.

"This ought to do the trick, lad."

The padre applied the key, which in reality was more of a wrench, to the manacles on my wrists. It took him a few moments, but in the end I was finally free. I stood up shakily and rubbed my chafed wrists.

"I suggest we beat a hasty retreat, padre. Conklin has a couple of plus sized minions named Siegfried and Hans or something that could be down here at any moment. I'm not sure that I could help you fend them off if they showed up."

"As they say, James, discretion is the better part of valor. I hope you learned what you came for?"

"I learned enough. But let's get out of here."

The window was a good seven feet above the cellar floor, but the padre managed to boost me up to it. It was a tight fit, but I managed to wiggle through and flop on the ground outside. I turned around to lend a hand to the padre, but he had already managed to get a purchase on the window casing and was pulling himself up and out.

"I believe you have an automobile parked in the neighborhood," the padre said, heading off in that direction.

The priest had obviously been keeping the house under observation the entire time I had been inside. I thought of bringing this point up with him, but decided against it as there was no point in doing so.

"How long was I inside?" I asked once we were walking down the sidewalk to the car.

"Oh, some six or seven hours," Donnelly replied.

I was surprised. I had no idea how long I had been out. For all I knew, it could have been there for days. "It seems like it was longer."

"I suspect that it did. Time always does seem to pass slower in jail." The way the padre said that made me think that it was from personal experience.

We got to the car and got in. My hands were a little shaky on the wheel, but I managed to get it started. I pulled away from the curb and drove in no particular direction, wanting only to get away from the temple. After a few blocks, the padre raised his hand and indicated that I should pull over.

"Now, James, tell me what you discovered," the padre said eagerly.

"Well, for one thing, Conklin is mad as a hatter. He really thinks that the codex contains the secret of immortality. He rambled on about druids and nonsense like that. I'm pretty sure that's what he's offered his henchmen to get their cooperation. He made me the same promise—if I helped him obtain the codex."

"Yes, I know all that, James. But the book, does he have the book?" the priest asked excitedly.

"He didn't act like it. As I said, he wanted me to throw in with him to get it. I don't doubt that Conklin and those two roughnecks of his would steal and even murder to get their hands on the codex, but I don't think that they were responsible for Levi's death."

"So that leaves us still in the dark as to the book's whereabouts," the padre commented. At the phrase "in the dark" I found myself shuddering. "Did you learn anything else of interest in that den of iniquity?"

"I asked him about Fenchurch's visit. Conklin told me that he had come to sound Conklin out as to what he would pay for the codex. Fenchurch claimed he didn't have it but that he thought he knew where it was."

"So Fenchurch is eliminated. We're running out of suspects, James. Anything else?"

"The American seems to be a non-factor as far as Conklin knows."

The padre paused while he considered what I had told him.

"I must say that I'm disappointed in the intelligence resulting from tonight's escapade, James. I had hoped for more. Still, sometimes what you find isn't so is as important as what you find is."

I found the logic of that statement a bit tortuous to follow, but that might have been due to the residual effects of whatever potion Conklin had put in the tea.

"What now, padre?"

"Oh, for the moment you can let me off on Mason St. I'll catch the cable-car from there."

The padre seemed intent on keeping his secrets. That was fine with me. What I needed was a drink and a hot bath. I drove down to the cable-car line and let the padre off.

After that, I drove the car back to the garage and turned it back in. The man on duty looked at the disheveled state of my suit but didn't comment. I didn't volunteer anything either. It was just getting light as I walked home.

I should have gone right to bed at that point. I hadn't had any sleep, I didn't count the time that I had been knocked out as sleep, since the previous night. But my body was telling me I needed food more than sleep. I fried up the last two eggs in the icebox, That and a couple of slices of slightly stale bread and a cup of coffee made a new man of me.

When I finished, I called Homicide to see if Lt. Miller was in. He was.

"Where have you been Tolliver?" Not the warmest of greetings, but considering the night I had had, I was glad to hear it.

"I was indisposed."

"What's that suppose to mean?" Miller asked grumpily.

"I paid a visit to Aleister Conklin at the Temple of Transcendental Enlightenment."

"How'd that go?"

"It was—interesting. He slipped a mickey into my tea, and I woke up chained to a wall in the cellar. That's where I spent the night."

"You don't say," Miller responded.

"Oh, I do say. When I came to, he questioned me about the codex. He was certainly keen on getting his hands on it, but I don't think he was responsible for killing Levi."

"What makes you say that?"

"Because he's still looking for the book. He tried to get me to work for him. He offered me immortality if I found it and turned it over to him."

"Immortality?" Miller asked in puzzlement.

"Yeah, and he didn't mean it figuratively. He was talking about living forever or at least a real long time."

"He wasn't serious, was he?"

"Oh, he was serious enough, deadly serious."

"The guy must be crazy."

"Mad as a loon, but that doesn't stop him from being dangerous. The thing is, he and his followers, he's got a couple of muscle bound types working for him, really believe in this nonsense, and they're likely to do almost anything to get their hands on the codex."

"What do you want me to do about Conklin?"

"I think it might be a good idea if you brought Conklin in and sat on him for a couple of days until I have a chance to find the codex. There are enough players in the game as it is. I'll swear out a complaint for false imprisonment if you want."

"Naw. That won't be necessary. From what you've told me I've got enough probable cause to keep a judge happy. You might need to come down and give a statement, but that can wait."

"That's good, because I'm about ready to hit the hay. Trust me, spending a night in a dungeon isn't particularly restful."

"Okay. Get your beauty sleep, Tolliver. Say, before I hang up, how did you manage to escape?"

"My fairy godfather broke me loose."

"What's that suppose to mean?"

"That priest I told you about, Father Donnelly. Well, he jimmied open the cellar window and broke me out. If it hadn't been for him, I'd probably still be stuck down there." I didn't add that if it hadn't been for the padre, I'd never have been in that predicament.

"I didn't know you were Catholic."

"I'm not. I was raised a Methodist, but I guess the padre overlooked that. By the way, why were you trying to find me?"

"I just wanted to let you know what we found on the butler."

"Which was?"

"Nothing. He's got no record in California. Nothing in New York or Massachusetts, either, at least under that name. Of course Stanley might be an alias—"

"It was a long shot, anyway," I yawned into the phone.

"Get some sleep, Tolliver. You sound like you could use it. I'll organize a raid on this temple place and let you know what we turn up."

"Fine. Call me in about twelve hours. I should be awake by then."

I hung up and went to bed.

CHAPTER 18

I woke up to a ringing phone. A quick look at the alarm clock next to the bed showed that it was five o'clock. A glance out the window told me that it was late afternoon and not the next morning. I hadn't gotten the twelve hours sleep that I had wanted, but I'd at least gotten eight. It would have to do.

The phone was still ringing, so I decided that I had better answer it. I stumbled out into the living room and picked up the phone and said, "Whoever this is, it better be important."

"Sorry, were you still sleeping, Tolliver?" It was Lt. Miller. He sounded almost cheerful at the idea of waking me up.

"I thought I told you to let me sleep for twelve hours."

"We raided Conklin's place. I thought you'd want to know."

"You didn't have to be so efficient about it," I complained. "What did you find?"

"Not much. Conklin and his cronies had flown the coup. It looks like they took all their clothing and personal stuff with them. They left a lot of Oriental crap behind, but nothing that looked like it was worth anything. I had the boys search the house from top to bottom for that codex of yours. They found a bunch of books including a crate of copies of Conklin's own works, but no eleventh century Irish manuscripts."

"That's too bad, Miller. I'm getting sick of this case. I'd just as soon give Brockington his damn book and be done with it."

"If you feel that way, why don't you just quit?"

"Because I'm no quitter. Also, I could use the five G's he promised me."

"Couldn't we all."

"Yeah."

"Oh, one other thing. When they checked the cellar they found the manacles that Conklin must have used to chain you up. Real antiques, right out of the Dark Ages."

"Yeah, maybe you can sell them to an antiques dealer," I suggested

"I had them entered as evidence," Miller said, ignoring the attempt at humor. "There were some suspicious bottles that I'm getting analyzed. Might be whatever they used to knock you out."

"Good luck with that. Whatever it was, I don't think it was regular dope. Conklin claimed it was some potion he found the recipe for in an old book."

"Whatever. We can get him on false imprisonment if nothing else. When you get a chance, come down and make a statement. There's no rush, though. There was enough uncovered there for the D. A. to issue arrest warrants for Conklin and the two others that were with him. Conklin left behind a bunch of papers, too. I've got somebody going through them, but I doubt if he'll turn up anything."

"Probably not, but there might be some things in them the limey police might be interested in."

"I'll keep that in mind," Miller responded. "So what's next?"

"A hot bath and a shave."

"I mean with the case?"

"You got me. Despite the fact that he slipped me a mickey and chained me up like a dog, I don't think Conklin has the book, and I don't think he was the one who killed Levi. That doesn't mean I know who did."

"That's what I figured. Well, have yourself that bath. Maybe it will improve your disposition."

I tried to think of something snappy to reply, but the line was already dead.

As long as I had the phone in my hand, I called the telephone girl at my office building to see if there were any messages for me. She said that a Miss Lanier had called several times and wanted me to call her back. I debated whether to take the bath first, but decided against it. Keeping clients happy comes first over creature comforts.

Stanley answered the phone when I called. He went to fetch Miss Lanier, and a few moments later I heard the warm tones of her voice in the receiver.

"I've been trying to get in touch with you, Mr. Tolliver." Somehow we had reverted to formal terms of address.

"Sorry about that, Miss Lanier. I was indisposed."

"Oh?" she asked with disapproval.

"Yeah, I spent the night chained up in a dungeon. It's okay, though. My fairy godfather came and rescued me."

"You're joking, aren't you, Mr. Tolliver?"

"Not really. I went to see a man about the case, someone whose name keeps popping up. Unfortunately, he slipped some drug into my tea, and when I woke up I was chained up in the cellar. He seemed to think that I had the codex, and when I persuaded him that I didn't, he tried to convince me to get it and give it to him. Of course, I told him that wouldn't be ethical. He left me to think about it and turned out the light."

"That sounds dreadful, Mr. Tolliver." There was an actual note of concern in her voice.

"It was. It was cold and damp and—dark."

"Are you making fun of me, Mr. Tolliver?"

"A little," I admitted.

"But you're alright now, aren't you?"

"I'm fine. I've had eight hours sleep and I'm about to take a nice, hot bath. After that I'll be raring to go again."

"That's good. Mr. Brockington is getting anxious about the codex. He's been pestering me about what progress you've made. I was hoping that we could meet, and you could give me a full report."

"Well, like I said, I'm about to take a bath, which, after a night in durance vile I could really use. But after that I could meet you for dinner. Say about seven?"

That seemed to surprise her, and it was a number of seconds before she responded.

"I'd like that, James. Where would you suggest?"

I thought fast. I wanted someplace decent, but not too pretentious.

"How about John's Grill on Ellis St.?"

"That would be fine, James. Seven o'clock?"

"I'll be waiting, Gail."

A little while later, while I was sitting in a hot tub trying to soak out the kinks from my night in the cellar, I tried to put together what I had discovered so far into something coherent. It wasn't easy. I had three suspects, Conklin, the American, and the padre, who by their actions could be ruled out of having the codex.

Conklin wouldn't have needed to put the snatch on me if he had the book. He could have just let me walk out of the temple without me being any wiser. Instead, he did something risky by drugging me and then trying to persuade me that it was in my best interests to help him get the codex. Of course, it was possible that he had been lying, but if that was the case his reasoning was even more convoluted than it seemed.

The case of the American was less clear. It was possible that having discovered I was snooping around in his direction he had tried to divert me by feigning innocence and then telling me he would be interested in making a deal if I did recover the codex. There was at least some logic behind that idea, but it just didn't feel right. It was much more likely that the American had been telling the truth and his offer to me was just his taking advantage of an opportunity that presented itself.

As for the padre? Father Donnelly motives were a lot harder to read. Sure, he had sent me into the lion's den, but then he'd come to my rescue. That whole play didn't make sense if he actually had the codex. It only made sense if the padre was as much in the dark as I was as to who had the codex and had been stirring things up just to see if something would emerge. There was also the fact that I was coming to like the priest. Sure, he was a rogue, but he was a likable rogue and not a bad drinking companion. I had no doubt that if the chance came up he'd hold me up for the codex, but I couldn't think of him as a killer. Whatever he'd been or done, I was pretty sure he took that commandment seriously.

So where did that leave me? Miller hadn't been able to turn up anything shady in the past of the Oscar Stanley, the butler, but that didn't mean anything. If he had a past, it might have been under a different name. But other than the old chestnut "the butler did it," there wasn't anything to tie him to the crime. This was real life and not some melodrama. There was no evidence to show that Stanley had either the skills to kill in cold blood or the contacts to fence the codex.

Which brought me back to the one name that had been lurking throughout the whole business, Edward Fenchurch. Sure, Conklin had said that when Fenchurch had paid his visit, the secretary had told him that he didn't have the codex, but that he thought he knew who had it. Of course, that could have just been a ruse on Fenchurch's part to protect himself. But did the fact that he had tried to shop the codex to Conklin mean that he actually did have the book, or at least knew how he could get his hands on it? Or had Fenchurch been playing a lower game, and knowing that the codex had been stolen, had he been trying to con Conklin out of some money with a vague promise? It wasn't as if Conklin would be in a position to complain to the cops. And, if he had tried that with Conklin, had he tried it on anyone else, the American for example? Of course, it was always possible that Fenchurch had been the one that had stolen the codex, and had been shopping it around trying to find the highest bidder.

I didn't have any hard evidence, but all my instincts were telling me that the man to watch was Fenchurch.

Having decided that, I got out of the tub. After a shave, I even looked almost presentable. The suit I had worn the night before was a lost cause; a night in a dungeon will do that. Fortunately, it hadn't been my best one, the one I was going to wear to dinner. I put on a clean shirt, dressed myself in my best suit, and after five minutes spent selecting an appropriate tie, I was ready for a night on the town.

It was still too early to head to the restaurant, so I called up the telephone operator at my office building. I was surprised when she told me I had a message. It was from Gene McCarthy. Given our last encounter, I wondered what he had to say to me.

I thought about blowing him off, but I still had time to burn, so I called the Hotel Alexandria. It took a few minutes to get him to the phone.

"What do you want, Gene? Are you planning to double-cross me again?"

"Don't be like that, Jim. What else could I do? It would have been my job if I hadn't."

"Sure. That, and a fifty dollar bill makes it alright, doesn't it? Anyway, you called me. Why?"

"Look, Jim. Maybe I owe you one. Not that any harm was done. But anyway, you asked me to keep an eye on who goes up to see the guy in the top floor suite, so I did. I think I might have seen someone you'd be interested in."

"What's the man upstairs going to say about that?"

"He didn't say I couldn't tell you anything. He just wanted to know if anyone came poking around him."

"I'm sure he'll appreciate that line of defense, Gene. So who did you spot?"

"I don't know his name, but I thought he kind of matched the description of the character you were interested in. He was thin, about five-seven or eight, thinning sandy hair slicked back. He had on thick, black rimmed glasses. He dressed real sharp, too, not flashy, but very neat and classy. Ring a bell?"

"Maybe," I conceded. The description sounded close enough to fit Fenchurch. "You say he went up to visit the man upstairs? Did he stay long?"

"Maybe half-an-hour. Are we square, Jim?"

"I'll think about it. If the tip pans out, we'll be okay. There might even be something in it for you."

"Thanks, Jim. You want me to still keep an eye out?"

"Sure. Look, I've got to run, Gene. I've got a date with an angel."

I hung up on McCarthy. His description certainly sounded like Fenchurch, so maybe the secretary was shopping the codex around. Things were looking up. I had a smile on my face as I walked out of the apartment.

CHAPTER 19

If you're not familiar with it, John's Grill is a place that's been in business since just after the earthquake. Its reputation attracts a diverse clientele who come for the good food, but the restaurant also has been known to attract more "colorful" characters that use the grill as a meeting place that is both public and private. More than one deal had been put together—or fallen apart at the tables there.

I had arrived early, and was nursing a Scotch and soda. When I'd been shown to the table, I'd taken the seat facing the front of the restaurant, mostly from force of habit, but also so that I'd be able to spot Miss Lanier when she arrived. I was glad that I did, because when she came in, it was a sight worth seeing. She was wearing an off the shoulder black dress with a white wrap. I doubt if the wrap offered her much protection from the elements, but it made a nice contrast that highlighted the graceful arc of her neck. The dress wasn't tight, but it did follow the contours of her body down to the black patent leather high heels on her feet. She had her hair up, not in a schoolmistress bun, but in a thick coil kept in place by a small, jeweled ornament in the shape of a butterfly.

More than one head had turned when she had entered, and more than one female companion scowled at the attention Miss Lanier was receiving. As the maitre d' escorted her to the table the heads swiveled to match her progress. I'm not sure what they thought when they saw me.

I rose as she approached, but the waiter beat me to pulling out her chair. After he had seated her, he gave a grave little bow and withdrew.

"I'm glad I picked this place rather than some chop suey joint," I said after I had resumed my seat. "Would you care for a drink?"

"I'd love one, James. A martini, light on the vermouth."

The waiter had arrived and I ordered, "A dry martini for the lady and I'll have another Scotch and soda."

"Very well," the waiter replied.

After he'd gone, Miss Lanier said, "I've heard about this place, but I've never had the chance to dine here. I don't have many opportunities to go out, I'm afraid."

"That seems a shame," I commented.

"Oh, it's not so bad. Mr. Brockington sets a very nice table, but most nights it's just him, Mr. Fenchurch, and me."

"Well, I hope the food lives up to your expectations," I said.

"I'm sure it will." Miss Lanier smiled as she said that, making me hope that she really would like the food.

We spent the next few minutes studying the menu. I'd picked up enough French during the war that I can handle most menu's. Miss Lanier didn't seem to have any problems in that regard. When the waiter came, she ordered a filet of sole. I had a steak au poivre with a baked potato. She suggested that we get a bottle of wine. I didn't disagree. The waiter seemed to approve.

While we waited to be served, we made small talk.

"Just how did you come to work for Mr. Brockington?" I asked. My interest wasn't strictly professional.

"I had studied art history in college, a fascinating subject, but unfortunately one with few opportunities for employment. I was working as a sales assistant in an art gallery when I answered an advertisement in the newspaper. It had been placed by Mr. Brockington. He wanted someone to curate his library. I applied and had an interview. He must have liked what he saw, because he offered me the position on the spot."

"I can see where he would," I said, regretting it immediately.

She looked up at me sharply, but ignored the comment. "The salary wasn't much better than at the gallery, but as it includes room and board, it was hard to refuse. There aren't that many acceptable opportunities for woman these days."

I replied, "I suppose not," hoping to make up for my earlier gaffe. She didn't seem inclined to offer further details.

"Do you travel much for your work?"

"Not that often. Mr. Brockington has agents in Paris, London, and New York that he uses for most of his regular purchases. Mr. Brockington can't travel much since his accident, and he does sometimes send me to the East Coast to handle the inspection and purchase of particularly desirable items. The Codex was an unusual case, of course, both from the nature of the item and the bidding conditions."

"Speaking of Mr. Brockington, just how did he come by his injuries?"

"It was a riding accident. I don't know all of the details. It was before I came to work for him, of course. About fifteen years ago, I believe. The horse fell on him and crushed his spine. I understand that up to that point he had always been a very athletic individual, riding, skiing, sailing, and those sorts of things. I think the accident has affected him more than just physically."

"Oh?"

"He's not a particularly happy man, James, despite his wealth."

"No, I don't suppose he would be."

"He's consulted dozens of specialists about his condition, but none of them have offered him any hope. He's even tried unorthodox cures, faith-healers and the like, but of course those are all charlatans."

The waiter interrupted us with the wine. He made the usual show of opening the bottle and offering a taste for my approval. As far as I was concerned, it tasted like wine. It was better than what I'd had in France, but then that had mostly been in shelled out villages in the Ardennes. I nodded my approval. Miss Lanier seemed to find the exchange amusing.

After a sip of wine she asked, "What about yourself, James? How does one become a private detective?"

"Pretty simply in my case. When I returned to the States after the war I needed a job. The National Detective Agency was looking for men who knew how to handle themselves and weren't afraid to do so. I bluffed my way through an interview and started working the next day. After a couple of years I was transferred out here to the coast. It was okay for awhile, but after a few years I decided I wasn't too happy with some of things I had to do, so I quit and opened my own agency. That, such as it is, is the story of my life."

"You say you didn't like some of the things you had to do. What do you mean by that?"

"We were hired in some labor disputes, strikebreaking, sabotage, that sort of thing. Some of it got pretty violent at times, and some pretty rough characters were involved. We did what we had to, I guess, but I got to feeling that I wasn't always on the right side. I don't have that problem now."

"You're always on the right side?" Miss Lanier asked.

"I'd like to think so, but of course you can't always be sure. In any case, I get to choose what jobs I take."

"And the Codex? You think that you are on the right side?"

I found the question odd.

"Something was stolen, and a harmless old man was killed. That seems clear enough to me."

I thought Gail was going to say something in response, but the waiter interrupted again by bringing the entrees. We ate in silence, enjoying the good food. I was pleased to note that my companion wasn't one of those women that pretend not to like to eat. Her table manners were graceful rather than dainty, and she matched me glass for glass on the wine.

It wasn't until the waiter had cleared away the plates and brought the coffee that we got down to business.

"Just what have you managed to discover, James? I'm afraid Mr. Brockington is getting anxious. I've never seen him so concerned before."

"Well, I have to admit that so far, I've mostly just been eliminating suspects. The American on your list is in town. I met up with him, but from our conversation I don't think he was involved at all. Not that he wouldn't entertain a chance to buy the book if it presented itself."

"But you don't think he was responsible?"

"No. Not even indirectly. There are a couple of other parties that seem to be interested in acquiring the codex, but from their actions, they don't have it either."

"Who are they?"

"One is an Irish priest. He claims that he's acting for the Vatican, and he might actually be telling the truth on that.

He was following me around for awhile. I guess he was hoping I'd lead him to the codex. He's an odd sort of character. Charming in the way the Irish can be, but there's a lot hidden beneath the surface. Thing is, he might kill a man, but I don't think he'd commit murder."

"Yet you say he's a priest?"

"That's his story. He's got some impressive looking credentials, but any good printer could have whipped those up."

"You said that you had had some difficulties—"

"If you mean being slipped drugged tea and waking up chained to a wall in a cellar, then, yes, I've had some difficulties."

"Was this priest responsible?"

"Only indirectly. He suggested someplace for me to stick my nose in. I'm not sure that he expected me to end up in a pickle, but he's also the one that got me out of it, so I guess I can't be too hard on the padre. No, the man behind that is named Aleister Conklin. He claims to be some sort of latter day druid. He's got a couple of followers that seem to have been sucked in by his spiel. He's interested in the codex for what he thinks he'll find inside it, and I'm not talking about the dirty pictures, either. He believes that the book contains the secret of immortality."

"Is he serious about that?" Miss Lanier asked incredulously.

"Serious enough to kidnap yours truly," I replied emphatically. "I've no doubt that he'd use violence to get his paws on the book, maybe even murder."

"But you don't think he actually has the codex?"

"No. That's just it. All three of the suspects I've mentioned propositioned me to cut a deal on the side if I should find the codex. The thing is, if they actually had the book, why offer me anything? No, when it comes right down to it, I don't think any of those three have the book or murdered Levi."

"Then you don't know who did it?"

"No. Let's just say I've got my suspicions."

"But you won't tell me?"

"What do you know about Fenchurch's background?"

"Edward?" Miss Lanier asked, surprised.

"Yeah. Mr. Brockington's secretary."

"Not much. I know that he's well educated. I think he came from a wealthy family out east. Connecticut, I believe. He was left quite a trust fund after his parents died, but evidently that disappeared when the stock market crashed. That's how he came to take a rather menial position with Mr. Brockington."

"Is he happy with that?"

"Not really. I know that he chafes sometimes thinking it's beneath him. But he doesn't have any better options. He and I are alike in that way, I believe."

"I'm going to ask you a question now, and I want you to know that I'm asking it as a detective and not personally. I don't really mean anything by it, but I still have to ask it."

"I'm not sure I like that, James," she said apprehensively, "but go ahead. Ask your question."

"Is there anything going on between the two of you? You and Fenchurch I mean."

A thin smile came to her lips. "No, there isn't. Not that he wouldn't like there to be. He's implied, in a gentlemanly way, that he was interested in me, but I've always declined politely. So, no, Mr. Tolliver, there isn't anything 'going on' between the two of us," she answered frostily.

"I guess I deserve that, Gail. I still had to ask the question, though. It's part of my job."

"I guess I can understand that, James. But why are you interested in Edward?"

"I've got a couple of reasons. One is that as far as I can see, heisting the codex was an inside job. Whoever did it knew when and where the book would be. They also had to have been known and trusted by Levi, at least enough that he would turn his back on them. There aren't too many people that fit the bill. Edward Fenchurch is one of them.

"The second reason has to do with that fellow Conklin that I was telling you about. I trailed Fenchurch to Conklin's Temple of Transcendental Enlightenment one night. He was inside for a half an hour, and I don't think he was there for spiritual guidance. Conklin said as much. He told me that Fenchurch said he didn't have the codex, but that he thought he knew where he could lay his hands on it. He was angling to see how much Conklin would pay for the book."

"I see," Miss Lanier said uncertainly.

"I have reason to believe that Fenchurch also made a visit to the American. You can't think of any reason that he might do so, can you?"

"No," Miss Lanier said, hesitating.

"Yeah. You can understand my interest. Now, it's possible that Fenchurch was just trying to pull a con and fleece Conklin out of some dough without actually having the codex, but you have to admit it is suspicious."

"And you believe this Conklin?"

"He didn't have any reason to lie. I was chained to the wall at the time, and in no position to do anything about anything."

"Do you actually think that Edward is capable of murder?" Miss Lanier asked.

"I don't know. That's why I'm sounding you out. Do *you* think Fenchurch is capable of murder?"

"I wouldn't have thought so, but in light of what you've said, I'm not so sure." In the dim light of the restaurant, I couldn't tell if this was a new idea for her, or whether she had wondered this before.

CHAPTER 20

The waiter came around and asked if we wanted anything more. By the way he asked it, I could tell that he was getting anxious to turn the table. When I asked for the bill, he had already had it prepared and pulled it out of the pocket on his apron.

After I had paid the bill, I offered to call for a cab and escort Gail home. To my surprise she said, "I'm not sure that I'm ready to go home, James. I get so few opportunities to get out. Let's go someplace for a cocktail. Someplace where we can dance."

"Suits me," I said. "Did you have anyplace particular in mind?"

"No, just someplace loud and decadent," she replied with a laugh.

This was a side of Gail that I hadn't seen before. She had shed the librarian persona for something more vibrant and wild. I liked the changed, but I wondered just how far it would go.

I hailed a taxi and gave the driver the address of a nightclub that I knew had a decent band playing that night. The cabbie just shook his head smiling as if he was wondering why some guys get all the luck. I couldn't say that I blamed him.

We could already hear the band playing a groove when the cab stopped to let us out. As we got out, the driver winked at me for luck. I tipped him an extra buck.

Inside, it took another fin to the headwaiter to get a decent table. I didn't care; it was Brockington's money.

After we had been seated, I asked Gail what she wanted to drink. She replied, "Oh, I don't know. Something exciting and colorful."

When the waiter came I ordered a scotch and soda and "something exciting and colorful for the lady." He just nodded in understanding.

When he returned a few minutes later there was something tall and pink on his tray. It had fruit slices on the rim of the glass and one of those little umbrellas. My scotch looked downright stodgy in comparison. Neither one of us had had more than a sip before Gail dragged me out onto the dance floor. I'm not much of a dancer, but fortunately, the band chose that moment to play something slow and quiet.

I wasn't thinking about the codex as we danced. All I was aware of was the pressure of my arm on her waist and the fresh sweet smell of her hair as she leaned her head into me. Time seemed to slow as we moved around the dance floor. The singer with the band went through a few verses then let the band play a few more before singing one more chorus before the end.

We weren't so lucky with the next tune, as the band switched to something up tempo. We tried to keep up, but it quickly became obvious that neither one of us was meant for the jitterbug, and we graciously yielded the floor to the younger members of the crowd, breathlessly retreating to our table.

"I haven't moved that fast since I dodged a German machinegun in the Ardennes."

"But you have to admit that that was fun, James," Gail said as I pulled out the chair for her. "I can't remember the last time I had fun," she added wistfully.

"That's a shame. Every girl should have some fun." I couldn't tell if Gail was getting sloshed or if it was just the flush of excitement. Up to then, she'd shown no signs of having trouble holding her liquor.

"The trouble is that every girl has to earn a living. Unless she has money, that is." There was a hint of bitterness to her voice that marred her beauty for a moment. "But let's pretend we have all the money we need, James, and enjoy this evening while we can."

She raised her glass and took a big gulp. When she set it down, there was a rim of pink froth on her lip. I couldn't help but smile.

"You don't smile much, James, do you? Not really smile, I mean like you're enjoying yourself. You should."

"Smile?"

"Enjoy yourself."

"Oh, I get by. You've mostly seen me when I've been working, which tends to bring out my serious side. Murder will do that."

"Haven't you ever wanted to be something other than a detective, James? Something like an artist or a poet? Or a musician?"

"I tried playing the banjo when I was a kid. I wasn't very good at it. As for being a poet or an artist, well, I hear the pay for those is even worse than for being a shamus."

"See, it all comes back to money. Don't you wish you had enough to just do what you wanted?" Gail asked.

"It would be nice," I agreed, humoring her. I wondered what had been in the pink thing. Gail was definitely getting tipsy.

The band took a break which made it easier to hold a conversation.

"What would you do for money, James? I mean a lot of it."

"Oh, I don't know. Just about anything legal, I guess."

"What about something that wasn't legal?"

I was wondering if that was just the booze talking.

"That would depend, I suppose. There are some things I draw the line at."

"Where is that line? Would you commit murder?" There was an excitement in the way she asked.

"No, that's one thing I won't do. Oh, I've killed men before, but it was always been a case of self defense or keeping someone else from getting killed. I don't think I could kill someone in cold blood."

Gail looked at me with those big beautiful dark eyes and said, "No, I don't think you could. This conversation seems to have taken a strange turn. It must be the alcohol. I'm not used to drinking so much. Would you mind terribly taking me home, James?"

"Of course, Gail. Anything you want." I settled up the tab with the waiter, and then we left just as the band was coming back up on the bandstand.

Outside the nightclub, I hailed a cab. I thought about just giving him the address and letting Gail go home alone, but considering her condition, I decided to make sure that she arrived safely.

The ride to Brockington's seemed to sober Gail up. She was very quiet as she sat in the back of the cab. When we got there, I asked the cab to wait and escorted her up to the front door of the mansion. She had a little trouble with the key to the front door, but I helped her with that.

"You won't get in any trouble with Brockington for being so late, will you?"

"I'll be fine. Mr. Brockington doesn't care for anything but his books. Thanks for being such a perfect gentleman, James."

I thought she was going to give me a peck on the cheek. Instead she kissed me full on the lips, a long, slow kiss. Then she opened the door and disappeared inside.

The cabbie had been watching the whole thing. When I climbed back inside he said, "Have a good night, buddy?"

"I've had worse," I said with a grin. I gave him my address and sat back while he drove me home.

I poured myself a nightcap of rye when I got home and sat for awhile. I was trying to make sense of the evening's conversation. Had it merely been the alcohol talking, or had Gail been sounding me out for something more? If so, what? She hadn't protested too much when I'd brought up Fenchurch as a suspect. Was that because she had her own suspicions? Or was it because she knew something about the secretary that she hadn't told me? I didn't have answers to those questions, and I was too tired to come up with them, so I went to bed.

I woke the next morning to the ringing of a telephone. It was mine. I tried to ignore it, but it kept ringing. After the fifth ring I finally gave up and stumbled out into the living room to answer it.

"Did I wake you, Tolliver? It's almost nine." The voice on the other end was that of Lt. Miller.

"I had a late night, Miller. Better than the last one, though."

"Must be nice," the lieutenant responded sarcastically.

"I was working, Miller. Interviewing Miss Lanier. Not that it's any of your business."

"Interviewing? Is that what you call it? I thought the two of you had dinner and then went dancing," Miller said smugly.

"Have you been following me, Miller?"

"Not you. Your girl friend. Remember, she's a suspect in a murder investigation."

"Don't you have better things to do with the public's money?"

"Don't get in a huff, Tolliver. I was just doing my job. Besides, she may be off the hook for the Levi killing."

"What's happened? Why did you call me?"

"I hate to say this, Tolliver, but you were right," Miller conceded.

"Right about what?"

"The butler. I had one of my men get his fingerprints. When I sent them back east, they found a match. Turns out your friend Stanley's got a record, only his name ain't Oscar Stanley. It's Samuel Oswald. He did a twelve month stretch for an armed robbery he did in Boston eighteen years ago. I had him picked up this morning."

"It's kind of a stretch from a stick up two decades ago to murder, Miller," I commented. The butler had seemed a long shot to me.

"Well, you haven't turned up anything better, and neither have I. Anyway, he's cooling his heels in an interrogation room right now. I thought I'd give you a chance to sit in when I question him. Just to show Brockington that I'm cooperating, you understand."

"Yeah. Okay, I appreciate that, Al. Can you give me half an hour to get dressed and get down there?"

"Don't rush. The butler ain't going anywhere, and the longer he sits waiting the better, as far as I'm concerned."

I didn't get a chance to say anything more, because Miller had hung up.

A quick check in the bathroom mirror showed me that I could skip a shave. The butler wouldn't care and Miller wouldn't notice. I put on a clean shirt and my second best suit and caught a cab down to Portsmouth Square and the Hall of Justice.

Chapter 21

Miller was waiting impatiently for me when I arrived. "Took you long enough."

"On the phone I said half-an-hour. It's only been twenty five minutes. When did you bring the old boy in?"

"There was a wire from Boston waiting for me when I got in this morning. I sent a car and a couple of uniforms out as soon as I read it. He's been sitting here since just after eight."

"Only two men? Didn't give you any trouble, did he?"

"Nah. He came quietly enough," Miller replied before he realized I had been pulling his leg.

"Has he confessed yet? Or haven't you brought out the rubber hoses?"

"If I'd thought you weren't going to take this seriously, I wouldn't have called you, Tolliver. After all, it was your idea."

"Sorry, Al," I said, trying to mollify the lieutenant. "It's just that I don't see Stanley or Oswald or whatever his name is as our prime suspect. For one thing, he probably doesn't have the contacts for fencing the book."

"Maybe he's working for someone," Miller suggested. I could see that he was operating on the old police principle that it was better to have a suspect in the hoosegow than two on the loose.

"It's possible, I guess. Maybe we should see what he has to say for himself."

"That's what I've been trying to do, Tolliver. Well, let's get it over with."

They'd stuffed the old boy into an interrogation room. Stanley was wearing his full butler rig, but with the addition of a pair of handcuffs. They had set him in a hard-backed chair in front of a plain wooden table. A desk lamp stood on the table, just like you see in the movies for the third degree except they hadn't turned it on. It didn't look like they'd roughed the butler up much bringing him in, but then he didn't look like he had put up much resistance, either.

Miller and I sat down in the two chairs facing him. One of Miller's men leaned in the corner behind Stanley ready to take a slug at him if he got out of line. I didn't think that that was going to happen.

Miller didn't waste any time.

"We know that you did a stretch for armed robbery out east, Oswald. Why didn't you tell us about it?"

"You didn't ask, sir." He answered in the same way he would have asked "one lump or two" when serving tea.

"You don't deny it, though, do you?"

"There wouldn't be any point in doing so, would there?"

"No there wouldn't," Miller said belligerently. "Does Brockington know you served time?"

"Yes, sir. I told him at the time that he hired me. Mr. Brockington thought he was giving me the chance of a fresh start. He was very good about it. That was before his unfortunate accident."

"Oh, he did, did he?" Miller asked.

I could see that the interview was going downhill fast. I jumped in before Miller could say anything more. "Why don't you tell us about it?" I asked, trying to sound sympathetic.

"There's not much to tell. It was right after the war. I'd been discharged. I didn't have a job or any prospects. My health wasn't that good because of my time in the trenches. I was desperate, Mr. Tolliver. Maybe you can understand that."

I hadn't told the butler that I'd also served in France, but then I didn't have to. He just knew.

"As I say, I was desperate. One night I took a pistol and held up a newsstand. It was a foolish thing to do. I got eleven dollars and fifteen cents. The police found me the next day. There wasn't a trial. I plead guilty because I was. The judge, when he found out I was a veteran, let me off with only a year in prison, which was kind of him, I guess."

"So how'd you end up as a butler?"

"I'd served as an officer's orderly during the war. It was about the only skill I had. When Mr. Brockington's was visiting Boston, his valet had come down with influenza and he needed a replacement. He discovered me through an employment agency. I interviewed and I was hired. I've been with him ever since."

"And you told Brockington that you'd been in the jug?"

"I informed him that I had a police record, if that's what you mean, Mr. Tolliver."

I had to smile at that. Not many men maintain their composure in a police interrogation room.

Miller was getting impatient.

"Enough with the sob story, Oswald. What did you do with the book?"

"Do you mean the Rathcael Codex, lieutenant?"

"Yeah. You know what I mean."

"I've done nothing with it, sir. I've never seen the codex. It never arrived."

"But you knew about, didn't you? Before it was stolen and Levi was murdered."

"I knew that Mr. Brockington was expecting the arrival of a valuable manuscript. I had overheard him discussing it with Miss Lanier and Mr. Fenchurch."

"So you were eavesdropping at keyholes, were you?"

"No, sir. I heard them discuss it over dinner as I was serving them, sir. One can't help hearing things in that situation. Mr. Brockington and the others made no attempt to keep what they were saying a secret."

"And what did you think when you heard about the book, Oswald?" Miller asked sharply. "Did you think that this was your big chance to get rich? Were you tired of being a butler?"

"I didn't think anything about it, sir. I've been quite happy serving as Mr. Brockington's butler. He's been an excellent employer, despite everything."

"What do you mean by that, 'despite everything'?" Miller asked.

"I mean, sir, about his accident. It was quite unfortunate. Things have been difficult at times with Mr. Brockington, which is only understandable. He was such an active gentleman before. But he has always treated me well."

"Yeah, yeah. Let's get back to the book. You knew it was valuable, didn't you?"

"I knew that Mr. Brockington had paid a great deal of money for it, but then he often had spent large sums on books and works of art. He has a great deal of money to spend."

"You knew, though, that there were others who wanted to get their hands on the book? Others who would also pay a great deal of money to obtain it?"

"I assumed so, sir. There usually are. I knew that Mr. Brockington had discussed his competitors for the codex with Miss Lanier. Before she went off to Europe to bid on it, that is."

"Do you know who these other bidders were?"

"That was a matter that didn't concern me, sir."

Miller was getting frustrated with the way the interrogation was going. I didn't want him to get off track. To forestall him, I asked, "Did anything strike you as unusual about the negotiations for the codex?"

"I'm not sure what you mean, sir."

"I know Mr. Brockinton bought any number of books and things. Was there anything special or different about this case?'

"Of course I wasn't involved intimately with the acquisition, sir, but it did seem to me that there was a certain amount of—shall we say—anticipation on Mr. Brockington's part."

"Do you have any idea why?"

"No, sir. I just know that he was impatient for the arrival of the codex."

Miller turned to me and asked, "What's this got to do with anything, Jim. Brockington had just laid down a bunch of cash for this book. Of course he was impatient. It's like a kid waiting for an ice cream cone. But Brockington didn't steal the book. He didn't have to. He owned it."

"Yeah, I guess you're right, Al," I responded. "Did Miss Lanier or Mr. Fenchurch share Mr. Brockington's impatience?"

The butler looked at me curiously. "There was a certain amount of excitement in the household, sir."

"Excitement?"

"Yes, sir. Mr. Fenchurch in particular."

"Was it the cultural significance of the codex that excited him or was it something else?" I asked.

"I couldn't say, sir," Stanley replied.

"What do you think of Fenchurch?"

"It's really not my place to say, sir," the butler demurred.

"But you must have formed some impression of the man."

Stanley paused thoughtfully for a moment. "I think that Mr. Fenchurch is a man with certain ambitions in life, ambitions that perhaps exceed his abilities to achieve them. Don't misunderstand me, Mr. Tolliver. From what I know, Mr. Fenchurch is quite competent at fulfilling his duties. I believe, though, that he was born with certain expectations of wealth which circumstances have prevented him from achieving."

"What's he saying?" Miller interjected.

"He means that Fenchurch was born with a silver spoon in his mouth that was yanked out when the market crashed."

"Why didn't he just say so?" Miller complained.

I didn't bother to answer that question because I assumed it was rhetorical. "Do you think that Fenchurch might have been tempted to steal the codex?"

"I couldn't say, sir," Stanley replied. "Though I believe he would welcome an opportunity to make some money."

"Why all the interest in this Fenchurch?" Miller asked me.

"Fenchurch knew when the codex was arriving and he had some idea of who might be interested in buying it. Levi knew him, as well."

"Oh, sure. Well, what about the dame, then?" Miller asked the butler.

"The dame?" Stanley asked, feigning puzzlement.

"I think he means Miss Lanier," I explained. "You'll have to excuse the lieutenant. His association with the criminal element has coarsened his speech."

Miller gave me a dirty look, but I was interested in what the butler had to say.

"Miss Lanier has always acted like a lady in my presence, sir. I believe, though, that her circumstances have also declined from those in which she was raised."

"So you think she might be tempted by what this book is worth?" Miller inquired.

"I couldn't say, sir. I am not a close confidant of either Miss Lanier or Mr. Fenchurch."

"Okay. Enough of this," Miller said in exasperation. "Let's get back to why I had you brought in. Where were you the night Levi was murdered."

"I was in Mr. Brockington's house. I've already explained that in my statement."

"Well, explain it again, why don't you. You were at Brockington's. What happened that night?"

"I served dinner as usual to Mr. Brockington, Miss Lanier, and Mr. Fenchurch. As was the practice, dinner was early. After dinner, Mr. Brockington retired. I cleared the table and attended to other duties."

"What about Fenchurch and Lanier?" Miller asked.

"After dinner, Mr. Fenchurch retired to his office. Miss Lanier was in the library for an hour or so and then went up to her room."

"Okay, go on. What did you do next?"

"I locked up the house around eleven as usual. Then I went to bed."

"Did anyone see you?"

"I believe Mr. Fenchurch noticed me as I went past his office after locking the front door."

"No one else?"

"No, sir. Not until morning."

"So you don't have an alibi from eleven that night until six o'clock the next morning. Is that correct?"

"If you mean is there anyone who can vouch for my whereabouts during those hours, then, no, sir."

"You have a key to the front door?"

"I have keys to all of the outside doors, sir."

"Does anyone else have keys?"

"Mr. Brockington, of course. Miss Lanier and Mr. Fenchurch have keys to the front door. The housekeeper has a key to the servant's entrance."

"So you, Miss Lanier, or Mr. Fenchurch could have snuck out in the middle of the night without anyone seeing you or them?"

"It would certainly be possible, sir. It is a large house with few occupants. All of the servant's quarters are in the rear away from the front door."

"Okay. No alibis for any of you. Tell me this, do you own a pistol, Oswald?"

"Yes, sir." I was surprised by the answer.

So was Miller. "You do? What kind?"

"A Colt .45 automatic. Mr. Brockington purchased it for me. For his protection."

"Do you know how to use it?"

"I was in the army, sir. I know how to shoot it—and hit what I aim at."

"Has it been fired recently?"

"Not in years, sir."

"Anything smaller? Say a .22 or .25?"

"No, sir."

After this barrage of questions, the lieutenant was running out of steam.

"You got anything you want to ask him, Jim?"

"No, I think you've about covered it."

"May I go now, lieutenant?" Stanley asked quietly.

"You can go when I tell you you can go, and that ain't yet!"

Miller got up and walked out of the room. Not having anything better to do, I followed him.

Outside in the hallway he asked me, "What do you think?"

"About Stanley or Oswald or whatever his name is? Not much. I don't think he did it, if that's what you're asking."

"I'm not so sure, but I can't hold him much longer without more evidence," Miller said. He ran his hand over what was left of the hair on top of his head. "I tell you one thing, though, I'd like to get a look inside Brockington's house, and I'd like to do it before I spring the butler. Do you think Brockington would go along with a search?"

"As long as you don't get too nosy into his private business," I replied. "I think he would allow just about anything if it got him back his book. What exactly are you looking for?"

"I don't know. Maybe a small caliber automatic. Maybe a wad of cash or a ticket to Tahiti. Right now, I'd settle for anything."

"Seems kind of thin—"

"Maybe if you approached Brockington—" Miller pleaded.

"Where's a phone?"

I called the house. Gail answered and got Brockington. I told him of Miller's request, and explained that if we did it informally without a warrant he'd have more control over where the lieutenant poked his nose. He agreed to the search as long as it was limited to just Miller and myself.

CHAPTER 22

Miller got a car with a uniformed driver, and we drove over to the Brockington mansion. In accordance with our agreement with Brockington, he had the driver wait in the car. When we marched up to the front door and rang the bell, we were greeted by the Negro attendant I had seen on my first visit to the house who seemed to be filling in as butler. A large man in his mid-forties, he seemed uncomfortable in the suit that had replaced the white jacket he usually wore.

"Mr. Brockington is expecting us," I announced.

"If you will follow me, gentlemen, Mr. Brockington is waiting for you in the library." Those were the first words I had heard him speak; his deep voice might have graced an actor.

We allowed ourselves to be escorted to the library where Brockington was at a table discussing some papers with Gail. He was using a wheelchair. I wondered if he had used crutches on our earlier encounter to make a good first impression. I introduced Lt. Miller.

"Is it really necessary to search my home, lieutenant? I would have thought it the last place for the thief to be hiding the codex." Brockington sounded almost petulant.

"We're interested in other things than the book, Mr. Brockington," Miller replied. "After all, there was a murder committed, as well."

"You can hardly think that Stanley is a murderer, lieutenant. He's been with me for almost twenty years."

"Stanley, or Oswald, has a record for armed robbery," Miller protested.

"Yes, yes. I know all about that business, lieutenant. I knew that before I engaged Stanley. He made no secret of the fact. That was a long time ago and a rather petty affair."

"I'm just doing my job, Mr. Brockington. With what information I have I could get a warrant, but Tolliver talked me into doing this informally."

"Very well. But I assume that you will release Stanley if you fail to find anything."

"If we don't find any evidence against him, I promise I'll see that he's released." Miller knew that he didn't really have anything that would justify holding the butler.

"Mr. Tolliver," Brockington said addressing me, "I'll expect you to see that this search is managed with a minimum of disruption."

"I'll keep an eye on the lieutenant, Mr. Brockington."

"Charles, please show these gentlemen to Mr. Stanley's quarters," Brockington said to his attendant.

"If you'll follow me, gentlemen?"

He led us to the rear of the house and up a flight of stairs to where Stanley had his quarters. It was a large room, quite pleasant, with a pair of windows providing plenty of light. The furnishings were of good quality if a bit dated, with a bed, dresser, wardrobe, and nightstand. There was a comfortable looking easy chair by the window with a lamp and table next to it. It looked like the butler enjoyed reading, because there were several books sitting on the table, one of which had a bookmark inserted. I glanced at the titles. They were both westerns.

"You can go now," Miller said to our guide. "We'll come get you if we need anything."

"Very good, sir," Charles said before withdrawing.

After he had left Miller said, "You take the wardrobe, and I'll take the dresser."

"Suits me," I responded. "Just don't make a mess of things. Remember, I still stand to make a bundle if I recover the codex. I wouldn't want to queer that."

Miller just grunted.

The wardrobe was an old-fashioned affair, with two doors opening into a large space above and a pair of drawers below. When I opened the doors, I found two suits, virtually identical, that were obviously Stanley's work outfit, and an empty hanger that must have been for the suit he had on. There was another more casual suit for use on his day off, though it was nearly as dark and conservative as the others. A dozen white shirts, clean and pressed were hung next to the suits. In addition, there was an overcoat, and on the shelf above a pair of black bowler hats. Six nearly identical ties were hung on a rack. Four pairs of highly polished black shoes were neatly arranged at the bottom of the cupboard.

In the top drawer I found several vests and a dozen handkerchiefs. The drawer underneath held several pairs of pajamas, a neatly folded bathrobe, and a couple of worn but serviceable cardigan sweaters. All in all, it was everything that the well dressed butler would wear and nothing more; nothing of a personal nature. I jumped up to look at the top of the wardrobe, but all I found there was dust.

Miller wasn't having any better luck that I was. When I glanced over at the lieutenant, he was pawing through an assortment of underwear and dark colored socks.

I moved over to the nightstand. I spotted a couple more westerns on a shelf underneath. None of the books were large enough to conceal the codex. It was when I opened the drawer that I encountered the first thing of interest.

Next to a bible and a flashlight was a gun. Just as he had told us, it was a .45 Colt automatic.

"Looks like I found his gat," I called out to Miller.

Miller came over to examine the weapon. He ejected the clip which was full. When he worked the slide he discovered there wasn't a round in the chamber. Stanley had been safety minded if nothing else. A quick examination showed that the barrel was clean.

"Hasn't been used in awhile," Miller commented.

"Too big to have been used on Levi, in any case."

Miller just grunted.

There was a small bathroom adjacent to the bedroom. It had a tub, a sink, a toilet, and not much else. The sink was a pedestal style with no place to hide anything. A glass with a pair of toothbrushes sticking out of it and a set of military style hairbrushes rested on the back of the sink. When I opened the medicine cabinet I found a bottle of aspirin, a cutthroat razor and a shaving brush, and a tube of some kind of foot ointment. For good measure, I lifted up the top of the toilet tank. All I found was water.

"If Stanley is hiding something more than a case of athlete's foot he isn't doing it in here."

"Yeah, well maybe he's smart enough not to hide something in his room. A house like this must have plenty of hiding places."

"There's probably a butler's pantry," I suggested, trying to be helpful.

"As good a place as any," Miller agreed.

We trooped down to the kitchen where the housekeeper directed us to the pantry. There was plenty of china, silver, and cutlery. There were also an assortment of various styles of glassware, bottles of premium liquor, and cocktail fixings. What there wasn't, was anything resembling an eleventh century Irish manuscript or a small caliber pistol.

"Any other bright ideas?" Miller asked. "With just the two of us, it would take a week to search the cellar and attic of a place like this."

"Gail mentioned that Brockington kept some guns in his study," I replied. "We might check that out to see if the collection includes anything smaller."

"Gail?" Miller responded with a raised eyebrow. "Just how close have you been getting to that librarian dame?"

"She came to my office to get a report of my investigation. Our dinner meeting was for the same reason."

"Whatever you say, Jim," Miller said with a smirk. "You know the layout of this mausoleum better than I do. Where's this study with the guns?"

I led him to the study. The guns were kept in a glass doored cabinet. They were about what you'd expect a rich sportsman to own. There were a couple of fancy double barreled shotguns that looked to have been custom made in England and probably cost as much as a new Chrysler. Added to these was a big game rifle and a Winchester carbine. None of them looked like they had been used recently. At the bottom of the cabinet were some drawers that were big enough to hold a handgun. Miller tried the door of the cabinet, but it was locked.

"I'll see if I can scare up a key," I said.

Gail was working alone in the library. She looked up and smiled as I entered. Evidently Brockington had retired to another part of the house.

"You wouldn't happen to know where there's a key to the gun cabinet, would you?"

"I think there might be one in the desk. Let me check."

She got up and walked over to a drop-front desk against the wall. I couldn't help watching as she moved. It was a sight worth seeing. She unlocked the desk and retrieved a key ring with a number of keys from a cubbyhole.

"I'm pretty sure that one of these is for the gun cabinet," she said, holding up the keys.

I had expected her to just hand over the keys, but instead, she walked through the door into the study. Bending over slightly, she started trying the keys in the gun cabinet's lock. I caught Miller eyeing her up as she did so. I can't say that I blamed him.

After a few attempts, the cabinet doors swung open. Gail stepped aside while Miller started pulling open the drawers. The first drawer contained some ammunition, mostly shotgun shells. The second drawer held a revolver, a long barreled .44 that looked like something out of the old west.

"I'm pretty sure this isn't the pop-gun that knocked off Levi," the detective said as he held the gun up to examine it. Out of habit, he was holding it by the end of the barrel so as not to smudge any fingerprints. "No bullets in the cylinder, and it doesn't look like it's been fired in a dog's age."

"Are you finished, lieutenant?" Gail asked.

"Sure. You can lock it up again."

After relocking the cabinet, Gail asked, "Is there anything else I can help you with?"

"If you don't mind my asking, Miss Lanier, just how many books does Mr. Brockington own?" Miller waved his hand at the bookshelves against the walls.

Gail smiled, "I'm not sure, lieutenant. I haven't finished cataloging the collection yet. But it's well over ten thousand."

"Any chance that this codex thing might be hiding amongst them in plain sight?"

Gail appeared to consider the possibility seriously for a moment. "I wouldn't think so. Mr. Brockington has been having me organize them by period and subject matter. I'm fairly certain that I'd recognize it if anything was out of place."

"I'm sure you would. Thanks, Miss Lanier. We won't keep you any longer."

"If you need anything, I'll be in the library."

After she'd left, Miller said, "Where next, Jim? Or are we done?"

"I don't know about you, Al, but I'd like to get a look at Fenchurch's office and room."

"You still hung up on the secretary?" he responded.

"I just think he's a more likely suspect than the butler. Besides, I never liked the guy."

"Does that have anything to do with Miss Lanier?" Miller asked.

"I don't think he's her type."

"Oh, I don't know, Jim. Some dames like intellectual guys."

I ignored Millers jibe. "Let's check Fenchurch's room first."

We had to go into the kitchen and ask the housekeeper for directions. She told us that Fenchurch's room was on the second floor at the opposite end of the house from Brockington's suite. She also mentioned that Gail's room was just across the hall. I didn't give Miller the satisfaction of reacting.

Fenchurch's room was on the front corner of the house and had been fitted out as a bed/sitting room with a pair of comfortable looking chairs in addition to the usual bed, dresser, and wardrobe. If anything, the secretary was neater in his habits than Stanley. The wardrobe contained a few carefully hung suits, a set of evening clothes, and assorted tennis flannels, etc. All had been custom tailored, though I noticed that none were particularly new. The drawers of the dresser held from top to bottom, handkerchiefs, scarves, and cuff-links, neatly pressed shirts, socks and underwear, and pajamas and sweaters.

It struck me has how few personal touches either Fenchurch or the butler had accumulated in their lives.

Miller was going through the contents of the night stand when he produced a cloth about the size of a hand towel.

"There's some kind of stain on this," he said. He brought it up to his nose to smell. "Some kind of machine oil—or gun-oil."

At that moment the door opened and Fenchurch walked in. "What do you think you're doing?" he shouted angrily.

CHAPTER 23

Miller turned to face Fenchurch, the piece of cloth clutched in his hand. For a moment I thought that the lieutenant was going to get rough. Miller is a big guy, and it wouldn't have been much of a contest. He probably had six inches and more than sixty pounds on Brockington's secretary. Instead, all he did was say in that flat official police voice of his:

"This is a police search in a murder investigation, Mr. Fenchurch."

"If this is a police search what is this two-bit dick doing here?" The two-bit dick was me; I've been called worse.

"Mr. Tolliver is assisting the police with the investigation. The department has been instructed to cooperate with Mr. Brockington's efforts to recover the Rathcael Codex. Mr. Brockington has been informed of the search and has given his consent, and last time I looked this was his house. If you have a problem with any of that I suggest you take it up with your employer."

Fenchurch looked like he wanted to say something, but he must have thought better of it because he just stood there with clenched fists.

Miller continued, "Now that we've gotten that all straightened out maybe you could explain this cloth I found in the nightstand. It looks like maybe it's been stained with gun-oil. Mr. Tolliver said that you told him you didn't own a gun."

Fenchurch looked nervous. "It's not gun-oil. It's machine oil. I was cleaning and lubricating a typewriter. You can check it yourself. It's down in my office."

"We'll do that, Mr. Fenchurch," Miller responded. "Right after we finish searching your room. I have to wonder, though, why you would put a dirty rag in your nightstand rather than putting it in the laundry or just tossing it?"

Fenchurch didn't have an answer for that. Instead, he asked, "Just what is it that you think you'll find?"

"We might find the pistol that was used to kill David Levi—or we might find the codex."

"Are you accusing me of murder lieutenant? Or theft?"

"I'm not accusing you of anything, Mr. Fenchurch. Yet. I would need evidence for that. That's why we're conducting a search. Now how about we take a look at that office of yours?"

Fenchurch didn't seem too happy with the idea, but he saw that there was no point in refusing. The three of us trooped down the front stairs to the secretary's office. Miller told Fenchurch to wait outside while we searched, but that just meant he was hovering in the doorway all the time we were at it.

The typewriter in question was sitting on a side extension of the desk. Miller gave it a long examination, though what he thought he'd find, I couldn't tell you. If he had had a magnifying glass on him I think he would have whipped it out just to annoy Fenchurch. Finally, he straightened up and started pawing through the papers on the desk.

It took us a lot longer to search the office than it had the bedrooms. There was a lot more stuff to sift through and more places to hide things. I noticed that Miller wasn't taking nearly the pains to be neat in his search as he had in the other rooms. The desk and the file cabinet were both locked, but Fenchurch produced the keys without complaint. Neither one of them was hiding anything.

Tucked against the wall was a good sized safe. It was a newer model with a combination lock. Miller tried the handle, but the door didn't open.

"You wouldn't happen to have the combination to this safe, would you, Mr. Fenchurch?" Miller asked, again in his inflectionless police voice.

Fenchurch came in, bent down over the safe, and using his body to shield his hand, worked the combination dial. When he was done, he swung the door open and stepped back out of the way.

The contents of the safe consisted of several ledgers, a number of securities, and a tin box with what I assumed was the household petty cash. There wasn't a gun hidden in it, nor an eleventh century Irish manuscript. There was an envelope marked "property of Edward Fenchurch." When Miller peeked inside he found a stack of crisp hundred dollar bills, ten of them.

"Care to explain this, Mr. Fenchurch?"

"Those are my personal funds, lieutenant. I put them in there for safe keeping."

"You know they have banks for that, don't you?" Miller asked sarcastically.

"I've learned to distrust banks. With good reason, I might add."

"It's a lot of money, Mr. Fenchurch," Miller commented.

"I've been saving for a rainy day," Fenchurch retorted. "Are you done in here, lieutenant?"

"For the moment."

"Then if you'll excuse me, I have *work* to do." He snatched the envelope out of Miller's hand and put it back in the safe. Shutting the door, he gave the combination dial a spin and made a show of sitting behind his desk.

"Thanks for your cooperation, Mr. Fenchurch," Miller said. "We'll let ourselves out."

As soon as we were out in the hall, Fenchurch shut the office door behind us. I heard the key turning in the lock.

"I can see why you were suspicious of that geek, Jim," Miller said. "I swear he's up to something, but it just might be cooking Brockinton's book. I doubt he came by that grand honestly."

"I agree, but we didn't find any evidence tying him to the Levi case. Are we done here?"

"Not just yet, Jim. We didn't look in your girl friend's room yet."

"Miss Lanier? You can't think she's involved."

"Just because she's a woman? I've run across too many of the so called fairer sex that would stab you in the back to give her a pass. You said yourself that Levi's killing was an inside job, and if it wasn't Fenchurch, she's the next most likely suspect. I think we've got to look at her room just to be fair about it. If it bothers your scruples you can stay down here while I do it, but I'm going up to search her room."

He headed toward the stairs. I wasn't happy with the idea, but I followed along behind him anyway.

At least when he was going through Gail's drawers he was neat about it. I made a conscientious effort searching through the wardrobe, even though I felt like a heel doing it. The dress she had worn to dinner was hanging there, along with a number of conservative suits, skirts, and blouses. Except for the evening dress, nothing was extravagant or out of place for a woman of her means. The same was true of her shoes which were mostly of the sensible variety.

Finally, Miller signaled that he was satisfied.

"Sorry about that, Jim, but you have to understand that I had to do it."

"Yeah, I get that. I'm just glad we didn't find anything. Are we done now?"

"Yeah. Let's get out of here."

Brockington was waiting for us in the front hall. He was still in the wheelchair with Charles behind him.

"Did you find anything, gentlemen?" he asked. He didn't sound put out or upset; more like he was anxious.

"No, we didn't," Miller replied. "I'm sorry that we had to put you through this, but we had reasons to be suspicious." Miller was trying to sound as courteous and conciliatory as possible.

"I understand, lieutenant. And I assure you, I'm more concerned with the recovery of the codex than any minor inconveniences. I trust, though, that as you didn't find anything that you'll see to Stanley's release? The household is hopeless without him."

"I'll arrange that as soon as I get back to the Hall, Mr. Brockington. And, again, I'm sorry for any inconvenience."

"Not at all, lieutenant. And please keep me apprised of your progress."

"I'll do that, Mr. Brockington."

Glancing back as we left, I saw Gail in the doorway of the library. There was a worried look on her face. I wondered what she was worried about.

"Well, that didn't get us very far," Miller said once we were in the car heading back to the Hall of Justice. He didn't sound particularly happy.

I replied with, "Oh, I don't know."

"What's that supposed to mean?"

"For one thing, there's that rag you found in Fenchurch's room. It's just the kind of thing you'd use to wrap a pistol up in, a pistol about the size of a small automatic. You have to admit that the line he gave us about using it to clean a typewriter was pretty weak. If he used it for that, why didn't he leave the rag in his office where it would be handy?"

"Okay, you got a point."

"The second thing is that grand he had stuffed in the safe. Someone in Fenchurch's position doesn't lay his hands on that much dough all at once, and the money in the envelope was all crisp, new C-notes. It's what you'd expect in a payoff—or an advance on something bigger."

Miller thought about that for a moment. "How much did you say that book is worth?"

"Brockington said that he paid thirty grand for it."

"That's a lot more than the grand we found."

"Yeah, but thirty grand is what Brockington paid, it's not necessarily what the thief might expect to get. After all, the codex is hot, and whoever buys it isn't going to be able to show it off. The thief may only be able to get ten or fifteen grand. Maybe less, if only one party is interested. The way I figure it, the grand we found might just be a deposit to keep Fenchurch from trying to peddle the book to someone else. Maybe that's what he was doing at Conklin's the night I followed him. He was trying to negotiate the sale and Conklin gave him a grand to keep him honest."

Miller pushed back his hat. "It's a nice theory, Jim, but we don't have any evidence supporting any of it."

"But at least you'll agree that Fenchurch is the most likely suspect."

"Maybe, but only because we haven't got any others. If it is him, what do you think he did with the book? And the gun?"

"If he was smart, the gun is probably at the bottom of the bay. As for the book, your guess is as good as mine.

Maybe it's someplace in the house. We didn't have the time or the manpower to search the whole place. It's more likely, though, that it's stashed someplace else, someplace that Fenchurch thinks is safe. Like a safe deposit box at a bank."

"You don't think that Fenchurch is working with someone and the confederate has got the book?"

"Would you trust something like that to someone else when it was worth that much?" I asked. "I don't see Fenchurch as the trusting sort."

"Okay. Say you're right, and I'm not admitting that yet, but say you're right, what do we do about it?"

"We keep an eye on Fenchurch. If he's got the book, sooner or later he's going to try to sell it. We just have to be there when he does."

"I can't keep a tail on him indefinitely," Miller complained.

"Then maybe we need to up the pressure on him."

CHAPTER 24

Nothing much happened during the next few days. I'd run out of leads to follow, and Miller was in pretty much the same boat. He had some men keeping an eye on Fenchurch, but Brockington's secretary never left the house during that time. Conklin and his crew had crawled into the woodwork. Even Father Donnelly seemed to be out of the picture.

I called Gail several times, ostensibly to report on my lack of progress in finding the codex, but really to sound her out on the possibility of asking her out for another evening of dining and dancing. She demurred each time claiming that she had too much work to do. Her attitude had suddenly turned cold and distant.

I had burned up a good chunk of the advance Brockington had given me paying bills and covering expenses, and with the prospects for recovering the codex dimming, I was reluctant to hit him up for more money. I wasn't exactly penniless, but if something didn't develop soon I'd have to start looking for some other clients to pay the bills.

The only piece of halfway good news was a call that I got from Miller.

"I hope you're having better luck than I am," I said eagerly over the phone.

"I guess it depends on your definition of luck," Miller responded. He wasn't exactly glum, but he wasn't bounding with joy, either.

"What's up? Something new develop?"

"Maybe. One of those names on that list of bidders on the codex that you gave me has arrived in town."

"Oh? Tell me more," I said, my ears perking up.

"Someone named Zoltan Tolkes arrived on the Hawaii Clipper last night. That's one of the names on your list, isn't it?"

I'd looked over the list so many times that I had it memorized. "Yeah, it's on the list."

"No telling if it's the same guy or not," Miller said. "I've got no idea how common a name like that is over there. Anyway, he's traveling on a Hungarian passport. Tickets on the clippers aren't cheap, though, so he's a possibility."

"Maybe you should bring him in for questioning," I suggested.

"The thing is, that passport he's using, it's a diplomatic one. He claims to be a count or something. I can't just roust somebody like that. Besides, he was on the other side of the Pacific when Levi was killed. I'd probably be back pounding a beat if I tried to bring him in."

"Any idea where he's staying? I might be able to approach him unofficially."

"On his customs form he wrote down that he was staying someplace in the East Bay, Berkeley, I think. Not a hotel, a private residence. Some friend of his, I guess."

"Any chance you could put a man on watching him? See if Fenchurch or someone contacts him."

"Out of my jurisdiction, Jim," Miller explained. "I can put a word in with the Berkeley police, but I'm not sure how much good that will do. The two departments don't always get along with each other."

"Maybe I'll go check him out unofficially," I responded. "A nice thing about being private is that I don't have to worry about things like jurisdictions."

"You do that, Jim, and let me know what you find out," Miller said before hanging up.

I didn't have anything better to do, so I took the ferry over to Oakland and then got a cab to drive by the address that Miller had given me. It didn't do me much good, though. The house was up on a hillside lot and I couldn't see much of it from the street because of trees and shrubbery. After staring up the hill for five minutes all I had for my troubles was a stiff neck. I gave up and had the cabbie drive me back to the ferry.

On the boat ride back to the Ferry Building I had time to think things over. At least two of the original bidders on the codex were in town, the Hungarian and the American. That might just be a coincidence, but it was also possible that the thief had been in contact with them. Into that mix I had to throw Conklin and the padre as well. With the exception of the padre, they all might have enough cash on hand to work a deal for the codex. I wasn't sure if the Church would spring for enough money to make the padre a bidder or not, but even without him there were too many players for me to keep tabs on.

Things simplified themselves a little bit when I received another call from Miller.

"What's up, Al?"

"Looks like we got ourselves a break. A patrol cop spotted the license plate of the car that you saw parked out front of Conklin's Temple."

"A roadster?" I asked, thinking of the car that Siegfried and his pal had driven up in.

"Yeah, that's the one."

"Where'd he spot it?"

"In front of a house out in Richmond. I'm headed that way right now. I can pick you up on the way if you'd like."

"I'll be waiting on the curb," I replied.

I opened my safe and pulled out the .38 automatic that I keep inside. I don't usually carry a gun on the theory that doing so is riskier than going unarmed, but in this case, I'd make an exception. I still harbored a grudge from my night in the cellar. I strapped on the shoulder holster I keep hanging on the hat rack, put my suit coat back on over it, and slipped the pistol into place. Then I grabbed my hat and overcoat and headed down to the street.

Miller pulled up in an unmarked car a couple of minutes later and we headed out Geary towards Richmond.

The house, when we came to it was quite a come down from Conklin's previous residence. It was a small, one-story bungalow, much like it's neighbors that had been put up to house the working class in the last dozen or so years. The small yard showed the neglect that seems to come along with short-term rental properties.

The same roadster that I had seen Siegfried and his companion drive up in was parked out in front, only this time there was a large steamer trunk tied to the luggage rack.

"Looks like maybe they're planning on going somewhere," Miller said, stating the obvious.

As we parked across the street, a patrol car pulled up with two uniformed officers inside. One of them got out and came over to talk to Miller.

"We've been waiting down the street for you, lieutenant. No one's come in or out since we came back from phoning in."

"Good," Miller grunted. "I want you and your partner to go around behind the place to make sure no one sneaks out. We'll wait for you to get in place before we knock on the front door. These guys are dangerous, so be careful."

"Yes, sir," the patrolman answered. He didn't look particularly worried by Miller's comment.

We got out of the car. There were three of us, Miller, the driver, and me.

"Do you want me to go up with you?" I asked.

"I don't see why not," Miller said. He had noticed that I had unbuttoned my jacket so that I could get at my gun.

We had just started towards the front door when it opened. Coming out was Siegfried carrying a suitcase. He froze for a second when he spotted us and then ducked back inside.

A moment later, Siegfried came out again, only this time he was carrying the suitcase in his left hand and a Luger in his right. I don't know what he was thinking; there were three of us waiting for him, all with our guns out. There wasn't much chance that he was going to make it to the roadster.

As things played out, he didn't. He raised the Luger and got off just one shot before the three of us shot back. At first I thought that we had all missed, but then Siegfried dropped the suitcase and stared down at his gun hand. He slumped to the pavement of the front walkway.

Miller was the first to get to him. He kicked the Luger out of reach. Blood was starting to stain the right shoulder of Siegfried's sweater. The lieutenant pulled out a handkerchief and was using it to apply pressure on the wound. Siegfried had broken out in a sweat, all the fight gone out of him.

About that time, one of the patrolmen that Miller had sent around to the rear popped out of the door, his service revolver in his hand.

"We heard shots, lieutenant."

"Yeah, blondie here tried to shoot it out," Miller said. "Anyone else inside?"

"I didn't see anyone, lieutenant. Kelly is checking it out to make sure."

"Somebody should go inside and see if there's a phone to call for an ambulance," Miller said.

When no one moved, I elected myself to make the call, and went into the house.

Like many bungalows, there wasn't any entrance hall. The front door opened directly into the living room. Beyond that, separated by a half wall of built-ins was the dining-room. A couple of bedrooms were off to the side. I guessed that the kitchen was in the back.

I found the phone on a table against the side wall of the living-room. I got the operator to connect me to the nearest police station. It took a couple of minutes to explain the situation to the desk sergeant and get him to send out an ambulance. He asked if we needed more men. I said I didn't think so, but that I'd check with Miller and call him back if we did.

While I was doing this, the other patrolman came out of the back bedroom. He nodded at me and I told him to tell Miller that an ambulance was on the way. With that taken care of, I decided to poke around a bit.

There wasn't much in the living room. There wasn't much in the dining room, either, but I could see from the way the chairs had been pushed back from the table that three people had been taking their meals there. In the kitchen, I found some plates stacked in the sink. Judging the few items of can goods sitting on the shelf and a half used loaf of bread on the counter, it didn't look like they had been planning to stick around long.

The back bedroom was the smaller of the two. It looked like Siegfried and his pal had been sharing it, though there was only one bed. I wondered if they had been sleeping in shifts or one of them had used the couch in the living room.

I decided it didn't matter. The dresser had been emptied, as had the tiny closet.

The bathroom was between the two bedrooms, accessible from each by a door. There weren't any toothbrushes or shaving gear in evidence. Conklin and his crew, whatever their intentions, had been planning to leave for good.

The front bedroom had been Conklin's. He hadn't left anything behind to mark it, but he had left an impression all the same. Again, the dresser had been emptied and the closet was bare. Oddly, the bed had been neatly made. I'd noticed the same thing in the other bedroom. Some English habit? I didn't have an answer for that, and I didn't really care.

I heard the siren of the ambulance coming up the street, and went outside to see what was going on. Quite a crowd had gathered on the sidewalk across the street, and Miller had set the two patrolmen to keeping them out of his hair.

"Find anything inside?" Miller asked when he saw me come out the front door.

"Some dirty dishes and a couple of cans of beans. It looks like they had packed up everything they had and weren't planning on coming back."

"No book?" Miller asked

"Nope," I answered.

Miller just grunted. The next half-hour was taken up with the ambulance crew bandaging up Siegfried and getting him onto a stretcher. According to the driver, the chances were good that Siegfried would survive. I wasn't sure that I cared one way or the other.

While we were waiting for the ambulance men to finish, Miller went inside and called the Hall of Justice to have a fingerprint man sent out. We twiddled our thumbs waiting for him to arrive. After he got there, we stood around another hour or more watching him dust things and take pictures. I wondered, why bother? We knew who had been staying there. Playing it by the book, Miller didn't want to touch anything until he the place had been checked for prints.

Finally, the fingerprint man finished and packed up his gear. As he drove off, Miller said, "Why don't we see what's in that trunk?"

I'd been thinking the same thing, so I agreed.

It took the two of us to manhandle it off the roadster's luggage rack. Whatever the contents, they were heavy. Miller had found a set of keys in Siegfried's pocket. He picked a likely looking one to see if it fit the lock on the trunk. It did. He unlocked it and swung it open.

Siegfried had packed as if for a long voyage. There were other things in the trunk besides clothes, though. We found a number of books, none of which was the codex. There were some oddments like a Chinese bronze knife and another one of silver which I assumed were of ritual significance for some of the magic Conklin claimed to perform. Packed away in a delicate little wooden box was the tea set that had been used to slip me the mickey at the Temple. There was nothing, though, that related to the codex or Levi's murder.

"That was a bust," Miller said in exasperation.

"What about the suitcase?" I asked, trying to cheer the lieutenant up.

The suitcase lock yielded to another key from Siegfried's pocket. Miller spent a couple of minutes pawing through the contents, but he only found Siegfried's clothing and personal items. The only thing interesting was what he found in a pocket of the suitcase. It was a steamship ticket.

"The *S. S. Santiago*," Miller read, "Departing Pier 35, 1:00 P.M. Destination Valparaiso, Chile."

It was three-thirty. Between the ambulance and the fingerprint man, we'd wasted a couple of hours. Miller ran into the house to phone the harbor master. From the look on his face when he came out, I could tell that he had been too late.

"The *Santiago* cast off right on time. Siegfried had been cutting it close."

"Any chance of getting them to turn back?"

"Not a chance in hell. The *Santiago* is registered in Chile. According to the harbor master it isn't planning on making any other stops in the States. They're out in international waters by now, so we're out of luck. The only thing I can do is send a wire to the consulate in Valparaiso to notify the police there, but that probably won't do much good. I doubt if the D.A. will try to extradite Conklin just for locking you in a cellar overnight."

As much as it hurt my ego, I knew Miller was right.

CHAPTER 25

I rode back to the Hall of Justice with Miller. It wasn't a particularly fun ride. The lieutenant was frustrated by the fact that Conklin had managed to slip through his fingers. I had my own personal reasons for wanting the magician behind bars, but I also recognized that Conklin had only been a peripheral player in the game swirling around the codex. It was obvious that he didn't have the book, and it was unlikely that either he or his two henchmen had had anything to do with the murder of David Levi.

As far as I knew, with Conklin eliminated from the picture, the market for the codex had narrow down to two, the American at the Hotel Alexandria and the Hungarian who was staying with a friend over in Berkeley. I didn't think that either of them had had anything to do with the original theft and murder. They had both been out of the country at the time of the crime. That didn't mean that they weren't interested in buying it as stolen property; the American had admitted as much. Of course, it was possible that there were other potential buyers, but if so, they were keeping a low profile.

It was looking more and more like I'd never collect the five grand Brockington had promised for the recovery of the codex. Miller was in the same boat as far as solving his murder case. Neither one of us was in a good mood, and the ride back to the Hall passed in sullen silence.

Things didn't improve much when we arrived back at Homicide. The D.A. had been in touch with the Chilean consulate. There had been an exchange of radiograms with the *Santiago*, the upshot of which was that it was impossible for the ship to return to port or dock at Los Angeles or San Diego. The next port of call for the steamship was Quito, Ecuador, but it was unlikely that the authorities there would be helpful. The chances in Valparaiso weren't any better. Conklin had successfully flown the coop.

The only cheerful note of the afternoon was that Siegfried had been treated at the hospital and the doctor had given his approval for him to be questioned. Miller decided to head over and asked if I wanted to tag along. As I didn't have anything better to do, I agreed.

Siegfried was being held in the prison ward. The doc told us that he would recover, but that his shoulder might never work quite right again. I'll admit that I didn't shed a tear over the news.

When we found him in his bed, the blonde muscleman looked pretty dejected. His good arm was handcuffed to the bed while his injured arm was strapped to his chest. He didn't look happy to see either one of us.

When Miller asked him his name, he just glared sullenly.

"Look, Siegfried," Miller explained, "you've got yourself in a big pickle. Your boss has left you to face the music while he takes a slow boat to Chile. At a minimum, you're facing twenty years to life for the kidnapping and the false imprisonment of Mr. Tolliver here, and your only hope of seeing daylight again is to cooperate. So let's start over. What's your name?"

Siegfried shifted uneasily in the hospital bed, the handcuff jerking him up short. "Siegfried Holst."

"See, that wasn't so hard," Miller continued. "Where were you born."

"England. London."

"How long have you been working for Conklin?"

"I've been a student of the master for three years."

"Okay. Now we're getting somewhere. Which one of you killed David Levi?"

"Who is David Levi?"

"He's the guy who owned the bookstore. The one who was killed when the Rathcael Codex was stolen."

"I didn't kill anyone. Neither did the master. And we didn't have anything to do with stealing the codex."

"If that's the case, why did you chain Mr. Tolliver here up in the cellar of that temple of yours?"

"I was just following the master's instructions," Siegfried answered sullenly.

"Do you always follow his orders?"

"He is the master."

"Would you kill someone if he ordered you to?" Miller asked insistently.

"I didn't kill anyone," Siegfried answered, a hint of hysteria in his voice. "You can't prove I did, because I didn't do it."

"But Conklin was interested in getting his hands on this codex, wasn't he?"

"Yes," Siegfried admitted grudgingly.

"Why?"

"Because it contains the Secret," Siegfried answered. There was a look on his face, the same kind of look I've seen on people in church.

"What secret?" Miller asked.

Siegfried looked at him like he was some hopeless lower form of life. "Why—the secret of eternal life."

"Eternal life, eh," Miller said. "That sounds sweet. I bet you'd do anything for it, wouldn't you?"

"I told you, I didn't kill the man in the bookshop. None of us did. We only found out that the codex was in San Francisco after it had been stolen."

"How did you find out?"

"A man came to the master. He said he knew who had the codex and that he could arrange it so that the master would get it."

"When was this?" Miller asked.

Siegfried gave a date. It was the day I had followed Fenchurch to the temple.

"Who was this man?"

"I don't know his name," Siegfried answered. "The master never told me."

"What did he look like?" I chimed in. "Slender guy, medium height, black rimmed glasses? Well dressed? A bit of a dandy?"

"That could be him," Siegfried conceded.

I looked at Miller. We were thinking the same thing, Fenchurch.

"Did Conklin and this guy work out a deal?"

"He wanted fifteen thousand for the codex. The master didn't have that much cash on hand. He asked for time to raise the money. The man agreed that he would hold the codex for a week if he was paid a thousand dollars as a down payment. The master agreed."

"Did he pay him the money during this meeting?"

"Yes."

"Do you know what form it was in? Was it in big bills or small?"

"I'm not sure," Siegfried answered. "I think it might have been in hundred dollar bills."

"During these—negotiations—did this man admit to having killed Levi?" Miller asked.

"No. All he said was that he didn't have the codex, but that he knew how to get it."

"And you don't know this guy's name?" Miller asked once again.

"No. I told you that."

"Yeah. Anything else you'd like to tell us?"

"The master didn't intend to hurt Mr. Tolliver. He just wanted to put him in a more receptive frame of mind."

"I'll keep that in mind when I testify against you," I said sarcastically.

Miller badgered the prisoner for a few more minutes, but he kept getting the same answers. Finally he gave up.

His last words to Siegfried were, "Don't leave town." Miller has quite a sense of humor.

Outside in the corridor Miller asked, "What do you think?"

"Me? I think he pretty much fingered Fenchurch. That's what I think."

"Maybe," Miller said slowly.

"Maybe? What's that supposed to mean?"

"He didn't actually identify Fenchurch, did he?"

"Fenchurch fit the description," I insisted.

"So does Harold Lloyd. It's not like we're talking about a man with a scar across his cheek or a peg leg. A well dressed man of medium height wearing glasses. That could fit a lot of people," Miller argued.

"What about the grand we found in Fenchurch's safe. Ten new C-notes."

"Maybe he closed out a bank account. Or he got the hundred dollar bills because it was easier to handle. It's not proof, Jim. And even if he got that money from Conklin, it doesn't mean he killed Levi or stole the codex. Maybe Fenchurch was running a con on Conklin. He knew the book had been stolen and he knew that Conklin was interested. Fenchurch cons him into forking over a grand knowing that Conklin is shady enough that he wouldn't go to the police."

"So you don't think Fenchurch is involved?"

"I didn't say that. There's a lot of circumstantial evidence pointing at him, but that's all that it is, circumstantial. I need a lot more than that to send him to the gas chamber."

"So what do we do now?" I asked in frustration.

"Now we wait and watch. I'll put on someone to watch Fenchurch and I'll keep tabs on the American and the Hungarian, too, at least as long as the captain will let me have the men."

"And what if nothing happens before you have to pull the tails?"

"Then I've got another unsolved case on my hand."

Neither one of us was satisfied with that answer.

Miller offered to give me a ride back to the Hall of Justice, but I declined saying I'd catch a cab.

Back at the office, I called Gail to report the latest developments in the case. Not that Conklin leaving the country brought me any closer to finding the codex, but reporting the fact gave me an excuse to ask her out one more time. I was hoping that she'd relent and actually say yes. Instead, she politely thanked me for the information. Unfortunately, she was busy and couldn't get away. It wasn't exactly a brush off, but I thought I detected a certain chill in her voice that hadn't been there the night we'd had dinner. Maybe it had all been wishful thinking, and I had been misreading her from the beginning.

I headed home, stopping on the way for a couple of drinks in lieu of dinner.

I went in to the office the next day mostly because I didn't have anything better to do. I was out of leads on the Rathcael case and out of ideas as to what to do next. If nothing came up soon to change that, I'd have to tell Brockington to save his money. I didn't have any other cases at the moment, either. Sooner or later I'd have to do something about that or starve.

I moped around the office all that morning. I read the paper that I'd picked up from front to back for want of anything better to do to pass the time. Nothing in the paper was of any help or even interesting. I thought about the bottle of rye in the desk drawer, but it was too early in the day, even for me.

I was about to call Miller and see if he wanted to drink some lunch when the phone rang. When I answered it, Gail was on the line. She sounded concerned.

"What's up, Gail?"

"James. I'm so glad that I was able to reach you. Something has come up that I thought you should know about." She was talking quietly, not whispering exactly, but speaking softly as if she didn't want anyone to hear.

"Has something happened?"

"It's about Edward."

For a moment I thought that I had blown the business and the secretary had vanished taking the codex along with him.

"What about Fenchurch?"

"He's asked Mr. Brockington for the afternoon off."

"Is that all?"

"You don't understand. Edward never takes time off. And he's acting strangely, almost furtively."

"Do you think he's up to something?"

"I don't know, James. That's why I called you. I thought you should know. He called for a taxi to pick him up at noon. If you hurry you might be in time to follow him."

"Do you think that's necessary, Gail?"

"I don't know, James. I just don't know."

"Don't worry, Gail. I'll take care of things. And thanks for calling."

Miller had said that he'd have a man watching Brockington's house, but I wasn't sure about that. I thought about calling the lieutenant, but I might waste enough time doing so that I'd miss Fenchurch. I decided to try to tail him myself.

CHAPTER 26

Luck must have been with me. A cab was dropping off a passenger just as I left the building. As I hopped in, I recognized the driver as one that I'd ridden with before. He knew that I was a private detective, which was just fine by him. He had watched too many movies, because he thought that what I did was glamorous.

"Sam, are you up for some excitement?" I asked.

"Sure thing, Mr. Tolliver. What did you have in mind?"

"I need to tail a guy, and I'm in kind of a hurry. I don't have time to get a car and drive myself, so I was hoping that maybe you could help me out. It may take awhile, but I'll make it worth your while."

"You can count on me, Mr. Tolliver. Where to?" Sam said cheerfully.

I gave him Brockington's address and told him to park down the street someplace where we could watch the front door. When I we got there, I looked around for Miller's man, but if he was there, I sure couldn't spot him.

We didn't have to wait long, because a couple of minutes later a taxi pulled up in front of Brockington's. A moment later Fenchurch came out the front door and got in the cab. As far as I could tell, he wasn't carrying anything that could be the codex.

I tapped my driver on the shoulder and said, "That's him, Sam."

Sam got the hint. He followed Fenchurch's taxi, hanging back far enough to not attract attention. It wasn't a particularly long drive, and we didn't have much trouble following. Fifteen minutes later, the cab stopped at the Ferry Building and dropped Fenchurch off.

"Thanks for the ride, Sam," I said as I slipped him a double sawbuck.

"Gee, thanks, Mr. Tolliver. You want me to wait?"

"No. It looks like I'm about to take a trip to Oakland, so I may be over there awhile."

"Well, thanks again. And if you ever need to follow someone again, I'm you're man."

"I'll keep that in mind, Sam."

As he drove off, he shouted, "Good luck."

I headed into the terminal where I saw Fenchurch get a ticket to the other side of the bay. I waited until he had moved off and then bought one for myself. If he was taking the ferry, I didn't have to worry about losing him for at least the next half hour, so I didn't bother with trying to keep him in sight.

The ferry ride was uneventful. When we reached the dock in Oakland, Fenchurch was one of the first foot passengers to get off. He headed straight to the taxi stand out in front. I followed, and when he got into a cab, I got into the one that was next in line.

"Follow that cab," I instructed the driver.

"Is this a joke, Mack?" the driver said turning around to face me.

"It's no joke, and there's a twenty in it for you if you don't lose it." I had a Jackson in my hand to show him I was serious. He took the hint.

There was a fair amount of traffic right around the docks, but it lightened up as we headed north. I wasn't particularly surprised when we passed into Berkeley, nor when Fenchurch's cab dropped him off at the house where the Hungarian was staying.

I told my cabbie to drive around the block and then find a place to park where I could keep an eye on the house.

"If you don't mind me asking, mister, are you a cop?" the driver said after he had shut off the engine.

"No, just a private detective. I can show you my license if you'd like."

"Ah, that won't be necessary, Mack. I was just askin'. Wait till I tell the missus that I drove around a private eye. She'll never believe me."

I found the driver's attitude amusing. People get all sorts of wrong ideas about private investigators from watching movies. As we were probably going to be sitting there awhile, I didn't want to disillusion him.

"Here, I'll give you one of my cards to show your wife."

"Gee. Thanks. James Tolliver Detective Agency. Didn't I read about you and that murder in Chinatown?"

"It's possible." I'd worked a case where the wife of a man named Mauston had wanted me to prove her husband had been murdered rather than committed suicide. It had gotten a lot of press at the time.

"Say, is that what this guy did? Murder someone?" the cabbie asked.

"That's not what I'm after him for. I'm looking for a book. I think he might have stolen it."

"A book? Is that all?" The cabbie sounded disappointed.

"It was a very valuable book."

"I guess it must have been if they sent a private detective to get it back."

"If it makes you feel any better, a man was killed to get it."

"Now that's more like it," the cabbie said enthusiastically. "You think this guy is the killer?"

"I'm not sure, but I figure if I find the book, I'll probably know who the killer is."

That seemed to satisfy the cab driver. He started pumping me about my exploits as a private eye. I filled the time telling him stories, some of which were even true. We were still going at it half an hour later when another cab pulled up in front of the house where the Hungarian was staying. A moment later, Fenchurch came down the hill from the house and got in.

I tapped the cabbie on the shoulder to get his attention. He started the engine and followed the taxi. I wasn't particularly surprised when Fenchurch was dropped off at the Oakland ferry dock.

I handed the cabbie the twenty and said, "Here's the twenty that I promised you. Say hello to the missus for me."

"Sure thing, Mr. Tolliver. And thanks again. This is the best fare I've had all month."

I figured there wasn't much point in trailing Fenchurch at that point. I took my time going about getting a ticket and was one of the last foot passengers to get on the boat.

After we had landed at the Ferry Building I watched Fenchurch get into another cab. I grabbed the next one in line. When I told the driver to follow, I felt like I was listening to a broken record. Fortunately, this cabbie wasn't very talkative. He apparently didn't go to the movies much, either.

I wasn't surprised when Fenchurch was dropped off at Brockington's. I figured that if he had had any other errands to run he would have done so, so I told my driver to take me back to my office.

I'd spent nearly three hours and fifty bucks in cab fare trailing Fenchurch, and I wasn't sure that I had anything to show for it. I knew that the secretary hadn't had the codex with him, because I would have spotted a package that big.

It was possible, even probable that he'd visited the Hungarian for the same reason that he'd approached Conklin, which was to negotiate a deal for the codex. That didn't mean that he actually had the book, or even knew where it was. Brockington might appreciate knowing that his trusted assistant was running a con game on the side, but it didn't necessarily bring me any closer to getting my hands on the manuscript.

I was thinking that the bottle in my desk drawer was looking more attractive when the phone rang. When I answered it, it was the padre.

"Where have you been? I haven't heard from you in days," I said. The padre had dropped out of sight right after my rescue from Conklin's cellar.

"Oh, here and there, James. You know how it goes," Donnelly replied. I wasn't sure that I did.

"Just why did you call, padre?"

"You followed that Fenchurch fellow today, James. It's possible that you might have been following the wrong person."

Somehow, I wasn't surprised that Father Donnelly had been watching Brockington's.

"Is there something I should know?" I asked.

"You might ask me where Miss Lanier went while you were chasing after Fenchurch," the padre answered enigmatically.

"Just what are you implying?"

"Oh, I'm not implying anything, James. I'm just making an observation, 'tis all. But you don't have to take my word for it, lad. You could give a call to that police friend of yours. A man of his was watching the place."

"If he did, he wasn't there when I followed Fenchurch," I objected.

"No he wasn't, more 's the shame. Or maybe not. If he'd been off following Mr. Fenchurch he would have missed the fact that Miss Lanier left to run an errand."

"What kind of errand?"

"That I don't know, James. But when she returned she was carrying a parcel. Now if you'll excuse me, I've got errands of my own to attend to."

I started to say something, but the line went dead. I knew that Donnelly was playing his own game as far as the codex went, but so far he'd mostly played straight with me in his own odd way. As much as I wanted to, I couldn't ignore what he had told me.

I called Miller.

"I thought you said you were going to have someone watching Fenchurch," I said when I was put through to the lieutenant.

"I did," Miller replied with annoyance.

"Well, he wasn't there when Fenchurch took a jaunt over to the East Bay."

"What time was this?"

"Around one."

"Give me a break, Tolliver. I could only spring one man for surveillance. He left to grab something to eat and make his report. He said he was gone for less than half an hour. How'd you know about it, anyhow?"

"A little black bird told me."

"That padre of yours, eh?"

"Yeah. Luckily I was tipped off and was able to tail Fenchurch. He took the ferry over to Oakland and then went and paid a visit to the house where the Hungarian is staying. The one on the list."

"You think he was trying to cut a deal for the codex just like he did with Conklin?"

"I wouldn't bet against it," I agreed.

"I guess that fits in with what my man saw. He just called in another report a few minutes ago, and he said he saw someone fitting Fenchurch's description pull up in a taxi."

"That was Fenchurch, alright. I was still on his tail. Did your man have anything else to report?"

"He said a woman left shortly after he got back from reporting. About an hour later she returned. He described her as good looking in a prim sort of way. Sounds like your girlfriend, Miss Lanier."

"Did he mention if she was carrying anything when she returned?"

"He didn't say. Just gave me the times. You don't think—"

I replied, "Right now, I'm not thinking anything," but that wasn't true.

Miller must have read my mind. "You said that someone tipped you off about Fenchurch going out. Was that your little black bird, again?"

"No. It was Miss Lanier. She called me to let me know that Fenchurch had asked for the afternoon off and called for a cab."

"Oh, she did, did she?"

"Yeah. Look, I'll talk to you later, Miller. Okay?"

I hung up before the lieutenant could object.

Gail had called me to alert me about Fenchurch, but had she done it because she knew I had my suspicions about Fenchurch? Or had she called me to make sure that I was out of the way while she did something she didn't want me to find out about? I had an idea what the answer might be, and I didn't like it. There was only one way, though, to find out.

CHAPTER 27

I had plenty of time to think on the cab ride to Brockington's. I couldn't help feeling that I had been played for a sucker almost from the beginning. But then I had asked for it. The beautiful dame playing hard to get at first, but then showing a vulnerable side that was calculated to tempt the private detective who was hard-boiled on the exterior but a romantic sap inside. It was a plot tailor-made for the inside of a cheap novel, and I'd walked right into it with my eyes wide open.

There was still a part of me that held out hope that I was wrong about everything, that the package Gail had been carrying held nothing more incriminating than laundry. Most of me, though, was convinced that that package held an eleventh century illuminated Irish manuscript. The only question that part of me had was how closely Gail and Fenchurch had been working together, and which one of them was calling the shots?

The cab pulled up in front of the house. I checked the .38 automatic that I had taken to wearing since the raid on the house in Richmond. The cabbie's eyes widened as he saw it when he turned to tell me the fare. I handed him a fin of Brockington's money and told him to keep the change. He didn't bother to ask if he should wait.

Stanley opened the door when I knocked. I asked him if Miss Lanier was in. He said that she was in the library. I told him that I knew the way.

I walked down the hall to the double doors leading into the library. Gail was standing at the big table. She was wearing a straight tweed skirt and an ivory silk blouse. Her hair was pulled back in its school-marm bun. Her tortoise shell glasses were perched on the tip of her nose. On the table, off to one side was a parcel that looked like it might contain a book. It was wrapped in brown paper secured by a length of twine. The package was ten inches by eight, and an inch or so thick, roughly the size of the Rathcael Codex.

Gail turned when she heard me enter. The look on her face wasn't fear, but it wasn't welcoming, either.

"James, I wasn't expecting you," she said. Her voice was flat with a hint of a chill in to it.

"I was in the neighborhood and thought I'd stop by and see you," I said. We both knew that was a lie.

"That was nice of you, James, but I'm afraid I'm busy at the moment."

"Oh, that's all right. I followed that tip you gave me about Fenchurch. You were right to tell me. I followed him over to Berkeley where he met with a man, the Hungarian on that list you gave me. I think it's possible that he was negotiating the sale of a book, just like he tried with Conklin."

"Oh? That's interesting. Did you want me to inform Mr. Brockington?"

"Perhaps not just yet, Gail. You see, I haven't quite worked out all the details yet, and I'd like to hold off until I've got everything in place."

"As you wish, James," she responded coldly.

I realized with regret that the woman I was talking to had nothing to do with the woman with whom I had had dinner and cocktails and then gone dancing with.

"I understand that you went out yourself this afternoon," I commented.

"Why, yes I did. Mr. Brockington asked me to pick something up for him. Normally Edward would attend to such things, but, as you know, he had the afternoon off. But how did you know?"

"A little blackbird told me. Is this what your boss asked you to pick up?" I asked, reaching for the parcel in its plain brown wrapping. It was heavier than I expected, heavier than you would expect a book to be.

"Why yes, as a matter of fact, it is. It's a new acquisition. Old, but not particularly valuable, I'm afraid."

I fingered the knot, but it was too tight to easily untie.

"Do you mind if I have a look? I find I've developed an interest in old books."

"I'd rather you didn't, James. Its condition is rather delicate."

I'd reached into my pocket for pen knife and unfolded the blade. The look on Gail's face was more of concern than anything else. For a moment I almost believed that the parcel contained nothing more than an old, valueless book. I hesitated, then pulled the twine taut and sliced through it with the knife. It parted with a twang. I began to unwrap the paper.

"Please stop, James," Gail commanded icily. I looked up to see the small, shiny, .25 calibre, automatic pistol she was pointing at me.

I turned to face her, setting the parcel back down on the table.

"I take it then, that this isn't just any old book, is it, Gail?"

"You know what it is, James." Her voice was cold and unyielding.

"Yes, I believe I do. Tell me, was this whole business Fenchurch's idea or yours?" I was counting on the fact that she wasn't going to kill me, but I couldn't be sure.

"Oh, James, you don't understand. You can't understand." There was a pleading in her voice, a pleading that made me wish that I did.

"Why don't you explain it to me?"

She seemed to be undertaking some internal calculus. I couldn't tell whether it was remorse—or something else. All the time, though, the barrel of the pistol in her hand didn't waver.

"It's not what you think, James."

"It seems pretty straightforward to me. You've got a stolen book, a book a man was murdered for. That seems simple enough. The only question is, which one of you pulled the trigger?"

"Do you really think I could kill someone, James?"

"It seems to me you're the one that's pointing the gun, Gail."

"Would you believe me if I said I didn't do it?"

"I'd like to believe you, Gail. I really would. If you won't tell me who killed Levi, at least tell me why."

"Oh, James. You have no idea what it is like. Both of us, Edward and I, our families had money, and then they didn't. We didn't grow up poor. We weren't used to it. And then to have to work for a rich man like Brockington as if we were servants—" She faltered for a moment then, the bitterness visible in her eyes.

"But then the codex came into the picture, an object so valuable that it would set us free if only we possessed it. Do you have any idea what thirty thousand dollars can buy?"

"I've got some idea, Gail. Mind you, I've never had the opportunity to see."

"At first it was just a joke between Edward and I. A child's game, imagining what you might do with a million dollars. But then we got more serious about it. It was still an intellectual exercise, you have to understand. But we started to work out the details; when we would steal it, how we would dispose of it, those kind of things. We decided that it would be best to steal the book while it was in transit. That way we wouldn't be implicated. And we had to find a buyer, of course. That was the hardest part. There are only so many individuals with the means and desire to own the codex. I had the list from the auction, but Edward came up with Aleister Conklin on his own. That was really very clever of him."

"It certainly was."

"We had it all worked out, James. But you have to believe that it was all strictly theoretical as far as I was concerned. It was a game, an amusement. A story we told each other around the dinner table after Mr. Brockington had retired for the night. I didn't actually think that we would ever go through with it."

"Do you mean to tell me that you didn't actually intend to steal the codex?" There was a spark in me, a spark of hope, that Gail wasn't really an accessory to murder.

"I never thought that Edward would go through with it, James. I never agreed to actually do it. I was surprised—and horrified—when he came to me the morning after the crime and told me what he had done."

"If you didn't intend on stealing the book, why didn't you just tell what you knew to the police."

"You have to understand," she pleaded, "I was in a terrible position. Edward and I had made the plans together. I was an accessory to murder. He threatened me,

James. He said he had done it for me. He said that if I didn't keep my mouth shut and help him sell the codex that he would tell the police that I had been part of the scheme right from the beginning, that it had been my idea. What could I do? Most of what he said was true. I didn't think that the police would believe me. I couldn't risk it."

"You should have taken your chances, Gail," I said. Even as I said it, I wasn't sure that I was right. Who would a jury have believed? Fenchurch or Gail? Juries can be fickle things.

"I admit, James, that I was weak. I gave in to temptation. Edward said that when we had the money we would go away together; go to someplace where thirty thousand dollars would let us live like kings and queens. You don't know how much I wanted that. Not with Edward, of course, but to have money and be somebody again. It didn't seem so bad a choice, not when the alternative was prison. I agreed to help him. I know it was wrong, but I did. What else could I have done?"

"Out of curiosity, Gail, where has the codex been all this time?"

"It's been sitting in a safe-deposit box at a bank. That was part of the problem. The box was in my name. I had rented it when it was all just part of a game. That's one of the reasons why I didn't think the police would believe me that I had no part in the crime."

"I see. And was killing Levi part of the game, too?"

"No! Of course not! The plan was steal the codex in the middle of the night when no one was around. Unfortunately, Levi was still there. Edward must have panicked and shot him. We didn't mean for anyone to get hurt."

It was a good story. I really wanted to believe her. It's just that a few of the details didn't add up. Like the rental of the safe deposit box. And counting on Levi not being at the store; Levi, who kept the only key to his safe on his key chain. The shop hadn't been broken into. If the plan had been to rob the place when it was empty, then why hadn't Fenchurch just waited until Levi had left? Some of her story was probably true, but not all of it.

"Look, Gail, I won't lie to you. It doesn't look good for you. Even with the story you've told me I think you'll have trouble with the police. Now, I can put in a good word for you, and maybe they'll accept the part about you not being a party to the murder. You'll have to do some time, but not as much as for accessory to murder. The best thing you can do is to turn yourself and the codex over to the police and give evidence against Fenchurch. I'll help you with that if I can."

The look Gail gave me was one of regret and pity.

"I'm afraid I can't take that chance. James. I'm sorry. I really am." The pistol in her hand was still pointed straight at me. I found myself wondering if I could get to the automatic in my holster before she shot me, knowing full well that I couldn't.

"I'd believe her, Mr. Tolliver." The voice was Fenchurch's. He was standing in the library doorway, a snub nosed revolver in his hand. "It's the only thing that she's told you that's true."

CHAPTER 28

As the pistol in Gail's hand wavered between Fenchurch and me I watched the expression on her face. I couldn't decide whether it was fear or hate.

"Edward, what are you doing?" Gail asked innocently.

"I've been standing outside in the hallway for the last few minutes. I must say, it's been interesting listening. I hope that you weren't taken in by Miss Lanier as badly as I was, Tolliver."

I replied, "I'm not quite sure what you mean, Fenchurch," stressing his name in the same way he had mine.

"I see my hopes were in vain. You're as much under her spell as I was."

"Shut up, Edward. You'll ruin everything," Gail said sharply.

"No, let him talk, Gail," I said. "I'd like to hear his version. It's only fair."

Gail turned on me with angry eyes. Her pistol was pointed somewhere between Fenchurch and me. I was sure that if Fenchurch had chosen to, he could have shot her before she had a chance to react, but he'd been taken in as much as I had. I didn't think that he would be able to bring himself to pull the trigger.

"It's quite an interesting story, actually," Fenchurch said, with the disdain of a jilted lover.

"I'd like to hear it," I encouraged him.

"It begins much the way Miss Lanier tells it, idle chit-chat around the dinner table. It will come as no surprise to you, Tolliver, that both of us were dissatisfied with our situations. We were, after all, born for better things. When we learned about Mr. Brockington's purchase of the codex, the idea of a windfall of thirty thousand dollars sparked both our imaginations. As Miss Lanier said, we began just by talking about what we would do with that much money. It was all very innocent at that point. Then we made a game out of how we could steal the codex without getting caught. One of us would come up with a plan and the other would poke holes in it. It was a relief from boredom, at least so I thought. I played along because, well, because I thought Miss Lanier was interested in me. Little did I know that what she was really interested in was having a 'fall guy.' That is the term for it, isn't it, Tolliver?" Bitterness dripped from Fenchurch's words.

"Yeah, that's the term," I responded. I could believe that Fenchurch had been played for a sap—just like I had.

"We even went so far as researching potential buyers. Miss Lanier came up with several likely candidates from the auction participants, but I was able to offer Conklin as a possibility. At the time, I was rather proud of that contribution. Of course, I didn't think I'd actually have the occasion to contact any of them. Then arrangements were made for the codex to be delivered. I found myself regretting the fact that our little game would be at an end. Little did I suspect—"

"I think that's enough, Edward," Gail said icily.

"Oh, no. On the contrary, I'm just coming to the interesting part. I'm sure Mr. Tolliver would like me to continue, wouldn't you?"

"I'm all ears, Fenchurch." I was wondering which of the two would break first—and how I could stay out of the middle of things when they did.

"Imagine my surprise when I discovered that the codex actually had been stolen. At first I thought that someone else had done what we had only imagined doing, but then I learned differently. Miss Lanier informed me that she had the codex and that she wanted my help in arranging for its sale. At that point, what could I do? The codex had already been stolen, and poor Mr. Levi was dead. I truly regret that part of it. That had not been part of our imaginary plans, and I always thought of him as a harmless old gentleman. Unfortunately, though, I wasn't in a position to disavow a role in the robbery. The fact was that I was compromised. As part of our 'game' Miss Lanier had brought up the question of how easy would it be to obtain a pistol, not to kill anyone with, mind you, but to use as a threat if the need should arise. I assured her that it wouldn't be difficult at all. To prove that point, I purchased that shiny little toy which she's holding in her hand at this very moment. I think that you'll find on examination that that is the weapon that killed David Levi. Fortunately, I had the forethought to purchase this revolver at the same time. The man at the pawn shop was most accommodating. He gave me a ten percent discount because I bought both guns at the same time. Unfortunately, there is a good chance that he will recall my purchase.

"You see, Tolliver, against my will I was made part of Miss Lanier's plot, an accomplice to murder. I couldn't tell the police what had happened without risking that I would also be charged and eventually found guilty. I had no choice to go along with her scheme. At least, if I did so, I might receive a portion of the proceeds of the sale of the codex. It wasn't a hard choice to make, Tolliver. Morally ambiguous, perhaps, but obvious. The fact remains, though, that it was Miss Lanier who convinced Levi to be at his shop that night, and who shot him in the back after he had opened the safe. I was home in bed at the time the robbery took place."

"Don't believe a word he says, James," Gail broke in. The shiny automatic in her hand was pointing at Fenchurch. If one of them shot at the other, I thought there was a good chance that I could get my gun out and shoot at the one that had fired. But which one would that be? I wasn't giving good odds on it being Fenchurch.

"I don't know, Gail. Fenchurch, here, tells a mighty convincing tale. I can see how a man's head could be turned by the attentions of a beautiful woman. But that was your intention all along, wasn't it? The dinner and the dancing? That was a nice touch, the poor young woman desperate for the taste of something exciting in her life. But you'd already had that taste, hadn't you?"

"I see that she got to you as much as she got to me, Tolliver," Fenchurch commented acidly.

"Yeah, I guess so. But then I'm just a two-bit shamus. I gather that that was my role in this whole business, wasn't it? I was brought in to handle the investigation so I could be manipulated at the crucial time."

"No," Fenchurch said, "that was Mr. Brockington's idea."

"Was it?" I countered. "And who suggested the idea to him? Why not one of the big national agencies, one with the manpower to be really effective?"

Fenchurch looked from me to Gail. "Why, indeed? Tolliver was your idea, Gail, wasn't he?"

"I don't know what you mean, Edward," Gail answered.

"Wasn't it you who suggested Tolliver to Mr. Brockington? Was your plan to have him brought in so you could seduce him and then at the proper moment persuade him to eliminate me?"

"I don't know what you're talking about, Edward," Gail retorted. She didn't sound particularly convincing.

"Let's get back to your story, Fenchurch," I interrupted. "The codex had been stolen and hidden in a safe deposit box. You started contacting potential buyers. Is that right?"

"Pretty much," Fenchurch conceded. "Our original plan, the one where it was all a game, had been to lay low for a period of time, say six months or a year, and then conduct another auction so as to get the highest price. But with the heat on because of Levi's murder, disposing of the codex became a higher priority. We were going to sell it and leave the country. That placed limitations on the pool of buyers, but that couldn't be helped. It was fortuitous that the American and the Hungarian buyers arrived in San Francisco just when they did."

"So neither of them are in town because of the codex?" I asked.

"Is there any point in rehashing all this, James?" Gail asked petulantly.

"I just want to get things straight for when I talk to the police. I wouldn't want to accuse an innocent party."

"No, neither of them were aware that the codex was available until I contacted them," Fenchurch answered, pointedly ignoring Gail.

"And Conklin?"

"Conklin was a bonus," Fenchurch said. "I had read something about his activities in the press. Given his reputation, I knew that he wasn't likely to go to the police."

"And the thousand dollars he gave you?" Gail looked up sharply when I asked that.

"He didn't have the cash on hand when I contacted him. The thousand dollars was earnest money while he raised the rest. Of course, I thought it unlikely that he would ask for it back if the deal fell through."

"Clever, Fenchurch. Did you get money from the Hungarian and the American as well?"

"Does it matter?" he replied.

"It might to Miss Lanier. Or did you know about the money from Conklin, Gail?"

"How much did you get, Edward?" Gail asked curtly.

"Isn't it too late for you to get self righteous, Gail? You were going to sacrifice me to the police. That was your plan, wasn't it? You'd get Tolliver or the police to kill me and leave them thinking that I had the codex hidden somewhere while you disappeared with it so you could sell it later when the heat had cooled down?"

"What if it was, Edward? Don't tell me you didn't have plans of your own."

"I guess there's no honor amongst thieves these days," I threw in just to keep things stirred up.

"Shut up, James," Gail said, turning away from Fenchurch so that the pistol in her hand was pointed back at me. "I should shoot the both of you. I could claim that Edward shot you when you confronted him and you shot back before you died."

"You'd do it, too, wouldn't you?" Fenchurch asked, shaking his head.

"Don't be silly, Edward. James is just trying to drive a wedge between us."

"That's hardly necessary, is it?"

"Oh, shut up, Edward, or I really will shoot you."

"I suggest you use a different weapon for each of us, Gail. It might raise questions if we were both killed with slugs from that pretty little pistol you have." I knew egging her on was dangerous, but it was the two of them that had guns in their hands.

"You seem to be forgetting, Gail, that I've got a gun, too," Fenchurch responded, waving his revolver in the air to reinforce his point.

"You'd never shoot me," Gail replied scornfully. "You aren't man enough. I don't know how you could have thought that a woman like me would be attracted to a worm like you."

I really thought that Fenchurch was going to shoot her then. He didn't. Instead, it was Gail who shot instead. The tiny automatic didn't make much of a bang, more of a pop, but Fenchurch slumped to the floor, a surprised look on his face.

It was almost as surprised as the look on Gail's face when she turned from Fenchurch to see the automatic I had pointing at her.

"I didn't really think you'd shoot him, Gail. I'd appreciate it if you'd drop that gun you're holding."

"You wouldn't shoot me, James, would you?"

"Do you want to take the chance, Gail?"

I could see her weighing her chances. Caution must have won out because she set the pistol on the library table next to her.

"Now slide it far enough away that you can't reach it. Carefully."

She reached out and pushed at the pistol. It slid a few feet, coming to rest against the parcel with the codex. I picked up the gun and put it in the pocket of my coat.

It was at that moment that the butler showed up, his eyes sweeping the room taking in the scene. I was half expecting him to say something like, "You rang, sir?" Instead, he looked at the pistol in my hand and asked, "Can I be of assistance, sir?"

"You can call the cops. Ask for Lt. Miller."

CHAPTER 29

I went over to check on Fenchurch, all the time keeping my eye on Gail. He'd been shot in the upper chest. A bigger slug might have done more damage, but the .25 automatic had been bad enough. I thought that he'd live, but for the moment there wasn't much I could do for him. I stood up and faced her.

"Looks like he's going to make it, Gail, which is a good thing. You'll only have to answer for one murder."

"James, you can't believe anything that he said, can you? That I shot that poor shopkeeper? Can't you see that it was Edward who did it?" Gail pleaded. She sounded like the heroine in a melodrama.

"It seems to me that you just proved yourself pretty quick to pull the trigger, Gail," I said nodding in Fenchurch's direction.

"It was self defense, James. He was going to shoot me. You can see that, can't you?" Her voice was shifting from melodrama to hysteria.

"I'll leave that up to the D.A. to decide, Gail. I don't know. Maybe you can convince a jury that you were just an innocent bystander taken in by Fenchurch's charm. They might believe you—" The way I said it made it clear that I didn't think so.

"Don't be that way, James. I thought we had something. Isn't there some way you can fix this? Make it all come out alright?"

"I don't think so, Gail. I've got to tell things as I see them. I'm just built that way. Besides, Fenchurch here isn't dead. He's not even dying. He's going to tell his side of the story, just as you'll tell yours. Me, I'll just fill in the details of what I know. As I said, they might believe you, but I wouldn't count on it. Juries can be funny, especially when a pretty woman is involved. You'd think that they'd be sympathetic, but most of the time it doesn't work out that way. It's more likely that a jury will think that the two of you were in cahoots together and fell out when things got tough."

"Oh, James. Please. We could leave now, before the police arrive, just the two of us with the codex. I'm sure that I could find a buyer for it. Then we'd have enough money to live like kings and queens."

"I don't think it would work out, Gail. I've seen what happens to your boyfriends. Besides, whatever you can get for the codex wouldn't last forever, not even in some tropical paradise where the living is cheap. One day it would run out, and then what would happen? Would you try to talk me into stealing something else? Or maybe kill someone? No, Gail, being a private dick may not make me rich, but at least I don't have to watch my back even when I'm in bed."

I thought she was going to say something more in an attempt to persuade me to go away with her, but that was when Brockington showed up in his wheelchair. He was holding the six-shooter from the gun cabinet, its long barrel looking dark and deadly. Charles, his attendant, was behind him pushing the chair. When he saw that Fenchurch was injured he went to tend to him. He seemed to know what he was doing, so I didn't interfere.

"What's going on here, Tolliver?" Brockington demanded.

"It seems that Miss Lanier and Mr. Fenchurch had a bit of a falling out and she shot him. Oh, by the way, I've found your codex for you. It's in that parcel over there on the table."

"The codex?" he asked. He seemed to be unconcerned about the fact that his secretary had been shot.

"Yeah. At least I think it is. I haven't had a chance to look at it yet."

"But it's intact? Undamaged?" He seemed desperate for an answer.

"As far as I know. I believe Miss Lanier has been taking good care of it since it was stolen." That got me a dirty look from Gail, but I was past caring.

"Miss Lanier? I'm not sure I understand, Mr. Tolliver."

"It seems that Lanier and Fenchurch have been scheming together to steal the codex and sell it on the side. I'm not sure which one actually committed the crime, their stories conflict on that point, but having stolen it, Fenchurch has been going around trying to find a buyer for it."

"And the codex has been in the house all this time? I thought you searched for it?" Brockington was getting himself worked up.

"Oh, the codex wasn't here until Miss Lanier fetched it today. It's been sitting in a safe deposit box since the robbery. I think she retrieved it because she was planning to take a trip."

"Is this true, Miss Lanier?" Brockington asked outraged. He waved the revolver around for emphasis. "Did the two of you betray me? After I brought you into my house?"

"And treated us like servants," Gail said. I didn't think it was the wisest response, given that Brockington was holding the six-shooter.

"But that was what you were, wasn't it? Servants, employees, they're both the same thing, aren't they."

I was getting a little worried about Brockington who seemed to be losing his grip.

"But, it's here, now, and safe?"

"Yes, on the table. You can see for yourself," I said.

He started to wheel his chair towards the table, making a mess of it because he still held his grip on the pistol.

"It might be better not to touch the book, Mr. Brockington," I, said. "I imagine the police will want to examine it. After all, it is evidence in a murder investigation."

"But it's mine!" Brockington exclaimed. "I need it."

"I'm sure that they'll return it to you as soon as they can, but they need to check it for fingerprints and things."

"But I can't wait for that, Mr. Tolliver."

"I'm afraid you'll have to, Mr. Brockington, but I wouldn't worry. With your connections it shouldn't be for long."

"But it might be stolen. Or damaged." His face had grown red and flushed. I didn't think that the excitement could be good for him.

"I'm sure the police will take good care of the codex. They know how valuable it is."

"You don't understand!"

"Understand what?"

"What the codex contains! What its secrets mean to me."

It occurred to me that to Brockington the Rathcael Codex was more than just a rare and ancient manuscript. Like Conklin, he had actually come to believe that between its covers were the secrets of immortality.

"You don't actually think—"

"Think, Mr. Tolliver! Look at me. I'm a hopeless cripple slowly dying in this damned chair. The accident robbed me of the best years of my life. Why shouldn't I believe? The knowledge in the codex will restore not only my legs, but my youth. Wouldn't you take any chance you could if you were in my place, Mr. Tolliver?"

I saw that the codex had become an obsession with Brockington. He was, in his own way, even crazier than Conklin had been. And he was the one holding the gun.

"When you put it that way, Mr. Brockington, I'm sure that the police will try to be accommodating."

"I won't let them take it, Tolliver. I won't," he exclaimed, brandishing the revolver. "You've got to see that they don't. You'll do that, won't you? After all, that's what I'm paying you for."

"I'll explain things to Lt. Miller," I said, trying to calm him down. "The lieutenant is a reasonable man." I was wondering what was taking him so long to get there. I wanted nothing more than to turn the whole mess over to him and get out of there. I found myself wishing I'd never heard of the codex.

"And these two," he said, using the pistol to indicate Gail and Fenchurch. "What's going to happen to them?"

"You don't have to worry about those two. They'll be arrested and tried for the murder of David Levi. Miss Lanier will maybe be tried for attempted murder on Fenchurch, but that's up to the D.A."

"And the codex? Will they be punished for trying to deprive me of the codex?"

"I'm sure those charges will be included in the indictment, Mr. Brockington." Actually, I wasn't so sure that the D.A. would bother, considering that he had a case of capital murder, but at that point I was willing to say anything to appease Brockington.

"That's not good enough, Tolliver. They should rot in hell for what they did. I should shoot them myself!"

He looked as though he might actually do it. He tried to stand, but the wheelchair rolled back, unbalancing him.

"I'm afraid I can't let you do that, Mr. Brockington," I said. I had brought out my automatic. I didn't want to use it, particularly on my client, but I wasn't going to let him shoot down two people in cold blood, even if they weren't innocent. I wondered again what was taking Miller so long to get there.

Brockington fiddled with the brake on the wheelchair, finally managing to get it set. He tried once more to rise, making it upright. Then he fell to the floor. The six-shooter went skittering across the floor.

I rushed over to him. His breathing was rapid and irregular and he was frothing at the mouth. His eyes had rolled up into his head. I was afraid that he had suffered a stroke or some sort of seizure.

"Charles, I think Mr. Brockington is in a bad way. You had better see to him."

The big attendant came over and gently loosened Brockington's tie and collar.

"How is he?"

"He's bad, Mr. Tolliver," the attendant replied. "His doctor should be sent for."

"Do it, or get Stanley to do it. Also an ambulance, if one hasn't been called for Fenchurch already."

Charles got up and went out into the hall.

When I turned back to the room I saw that Gail was edging over towards where the codex lay on the table.

"I wouldn't do that, Gail," I said, pointing the automatic at her.

"You wouldn't shoot me, would you, James?"

"I'm afraid I would, Gail. I'm afraid I would," I replied with resignation.

She must have believed me, for she dropped her eyes and moved back.

I could hear sounds coming from the hallway, the front door opening, muted voices and heavy footsteps. I looked over my shoulder to see Lt. Miller framed in the doorway backed by a couple of uniforms.

"What's going on here, Jim?" Miller demanded.

"It's about time you got here, Al."

CHAPTER 30

"I came as soon as I got the call from that butler fellow. Now tell me what's been going on."

"Where should I begin, Al. Miss Lanier fetched the codex from the safe deposit box where she's been hiding it since the robbery. It's in that parcel on the table. Miss Lanier and Fenchurch had a disagreement and she shot him. I've got her gun in my pocket. I can't be certain, but I'm betting that it's the one that killed Levi. By the way, I think Fenchurch will live if he gets to a doctor quick enough. While we're talking about doctors, you might see about getting one for Brockington. He's had some sort of fit. Good thing he did, because otherwise he was going to shoot Lanier and Fenchurch. I think that pretty much covers it. Any questions?"

"Plenty, but they can wait," Miller said. He turned to the two cops with him and ordered, "One of you get the cuffs on the dame and the other one find a phone and call for a matron. We'll probably need another car and a couple of more men, as well."

There was the sound of an ambulance pulling up out front and a few moments later two men came in with a stretcher. They debated whether to deal with Fenchurch or Brockington first, but were saved from having to make that decision by the arrival of Brockington's own doctor. He hovered over the millionaire for the next few minutes, the concern evident on his face. With Charles's assistance, he managed to get Brockington back in his chair and wheel him out of the library.

After that, there was an hour or so of the usual crime scene confusion while Fenchurch was carted off to the hospital and Gail was taken off to the Hall of Justice. The fingerprint men came and pictures were taken. A couple of reporters tried to bust in, but Miller shoed them out again. I thought about Shorty Smith, but decided I'd have to wait until later to fill him in on all the juicy details.

Finally, though, just Miller and I were left in the room.

"So that's the famous codex thing that this whole mess is about," Miller said fingering the parcel on the table. "Doesn't look like much, does it?"

"No, I suppose it doesn't," I agreed.

Miller grunted. "So what's the real story, Jim?"

"It depends on who you listen to. Miss Lanier says that it was all Fenchurch's doing. She never thought he'd go through with stealing the codex and she had nothing to do with Levi's murder."

"I see," Miller said. "And Fenchurch? What did he have to say?"

"Oh, pretty much the same thing, except that it was all Miss Lanier's idea and she was the one that killed Levi."

"And what do you think, Jim?"

"Me? I don't have an opinion. I'll leave it up to the D.A. to decide. I was paid to recover the codex, and that's what I've done. It's someone else's job to sort out the rest."

"Yeah, yeah. But just between you and me, Jim, who done it?" Miller persisted.

"Well, I never liked Fenchurch and he was the one that was shopping the codex around to potential buyers. But Miss Lanier was the one who had the codex and the one who shot Fenchurch more or less in cold blood."

"You were sweet on her, weren't you, Jim? Not that I blame you, mind. Behind those glasses of hers she's a pretty good looking dame."

"Maybe," I conceded, "just for a moment."

"Well, you wouldn't be the first guy to have his judgment clouded by something in a skirt," the lieutenant responded in a consoling tone.

"When you put it that way, you make me sound like a sap, Al."

"Well, weren't you? You kept insisting that Fenchurch was the one when almost everything you said about him was equally true of the dame."

I didn't really have a response to that, because I knew Miller was right.

"So what happened here? I need something to put down in my report."

"When I found out that Miss Lanier had gone out while I was tailing Fenchurch and had come back with a package, I came here to confront her about it. She denied it until I started to unwrap the package. Then she pulled a gun on me, a .25 automatic. She gave me a sob story proclaiming her innocence and blaming Fenchurch for getting her into this mess. She said that they had talked about stealing the codex, but that it had all been pretend, a game. Then she said Fenchurch went ahead and did it. Evidently, Fenchurch had been out in the hall listening most of the time. He came in brandishing a .38 police special. He confirmed everything up to the robbery. He claimed that he had never planned to go through with it, and that it was Miss Lanier who had stolen the codex and shot Levi. They argued for a bit, insulting each other, and then she shot him."

"Just like that?"

"Yeah, just like that. I have to admit, that caught me by surprise, but it gave me a chance to get the drop on her. I got her to drop the gun. That's when I had the butler call you."

"And Brockington? How does he figure into all this, and what happened to him?"

"He came in after Fenchurch had been shot holding that wild-west piece of iron in his hand. All he was concerned about was the book. Frankly, I think he is as crazy as Conklin. He actually seems to think that the codex contains a secret that would give him back the use of his legs and all the years that he's spent confined to a wheelchair. He worked himself up into some kind of fit. When he tried to stand, he collapsed. You'll have to ask his doctor why, not that it matters. That's when you burst in, as usual, just a little too late."

"Well, I didn't have the inside dope like you, Jim. That about it?"

"Pretty much."

"You'll need to come down to the Hall sometime tomorrow and make an official statement with all the details, but I think that will be enough for now."

"Okay. Let me know when you want me."

"I'll do that. And Jim, don't feel too bad. All of us make mistakes about people, particularly dames."

"Yeah," I replied. There didn't seem to be much more to say.

"I'd better go see what's up with Brockington," Miller said as he left the room.

That left me alone in the library wondering if it had all been worth it. Brockington had gotten what he wanted, but it didn't look like it would end up doing him much good. It was likely that Gail and Fenchurch would spend time in prison if not worse. And me? I'd burned through most of the money Brockington had paid me, and I had my doubts about whether I'd ever see the five thousand he'd promised me if I recovered the codex, so I wasn't in any better shape than when I had started the case.

Miller was right about Gail, too. I had made myself a sap over her. She had played me like a fiddle, just as she had done with Fenchurch. There had been a moment, though, out on the dance floor, when I had held her close as we swayed to the music that it had seemed as though there was something there, something real. Could it have worked out if the two of us had met under different circumstances? But if the circumstances had been different, would we have ever met at all? Probably not. Two-bit shamuses don't meet women like that unless they're in trouble—or are trouble.

What I needed was a drink. I wondered where Stanley was, and if he might rustle something up in that line.

I heard footsteps in the hallway, footsteps that were too quiet to be Miller or any of the other flatfeet roaming the place. I thought maybe my prayers had been answered and it was the butler.

I glanced up at a dark form in the doorway. It was the padre, and he was holding a Luger in his hand.

CHAPTER 31

"I've been wondering when you were going to make an entrance, padre," I said. "This business wouldn't be complete without you."

Father Donnelly made a little bow. The Luger in his hand didn't waver. "I'd rather not have to shoot you, James."

"I'd just as soon you didn't have to shoot me, either," I replied.

The glint in the padre's eye didn't hint at malevolence, but I didn't have any doubt about his resolve.

"I'll take that pistol that you've got underneath your jacket, James. That way we won't risk any unpleasantness. Just remove it carefully, please, and place it on the table, will you."

I did as the padre asked. I didn't see any reason to mention the automatic I had stuffed into my pocket.

"I suppose you've come for the book?" I asked.

"That would be it, James. I hope you won't put up a fuss about it."

"I never argue with a man holding a gun on me. That's it over there on the table." I gestured in the direction of the half unwrapped parcel. "I don't suppose it really matters one way or the other. It doesn't look like Brockington is in any shape to care."

"I'm glad you're being sensible about this, James. You understand that I bear you no ill will. In fact, I've grown rather fond of you, my boy. I'm just doing my job."

"Oh, I get that, padre. Though you do seem to be playing fast and loose with one of the commandments. 'Thou shalt not steal,' isn't that the way it goes?"

"It's not really stealing, James, is it?" the padre said with a wink. "After all, the codex does belong in the Vatican Library."

"If that's the case, padre, why not let the courts decide the matter?"

"It's like this, James. I'm not a great one for trusting the law. Besides, any court proceedings would be bound to involve a great deal of publicity. My superiors would much prefer that things were handled discretely, so I think I'll just grab the book and be off with me."

"Well, like I said, you're the man with the gun. Just one thing, though, padre. In this whole business, I never had a chance to look at the codex. I wouldn't mind seeing what all the fuss was about before you steal away with it. I don't suppose that once it's back in the Vatican it will ever be put on public display?"

"No, I shouldn't imagine that it will, James. Well, I don't see any harm in your having a peek. After all, you have been quite a help to me, James. I admit I'm a wee bit curious myself."

"May I?"

A gesture of the padre's pistol indicated his assent. I unwrapped the paper from the parcel. It didn't take an expert to tell that the codex was ancient. The dark leather had a dry, brittle look to it that spoke of its age. It was much as Gail had described it, ten by eight inches and a little over an inch thick. The pages looked thicker than they would be if they had been of paper. On neither the thick board cover or the spine was there a title.

Carefully, I opened the cover which turned back reluctantly. The first page was much as it had looked in the photo that I had been shown. What the photo hadn't revealed was the vibrancy of the colors. The inks that had been used were green, red, blue, black and vermillion, their brilliance undiminished by their age. The first letter had been enlarged and illuminated with applied gold leaf. The illustration, despite the nature of the subject matter, was the work of a true artist.

I noticed that the padre had leaned over me to get a better look, his Luger pointed in some indeterminate direction.

"Shall I go on to the next page, padre?" I asked.

"Please do, James."

I turned the page, then the next, then a third. They were all blank. I continued to turn the leaves of the codex, but except for the first, all the sheets of vellum were blank. Donnelly grabbed the manuscript from the table and riffled through the pages, a look of consternation on his face.

All I could do was laugh, not a chuckle, but a deep belly laugh.

"Looks like we've all been snookered, padre. You, me, Fenchurch, Miss Lanier, Brockington, the whole lot of us have been chasing after a fraud."

The padre set the book down and crossed himself. "Saints preserve us. I wasn't expecting this, James."

"Maybe it's a miracle," I suggested with a grin.

"Don't jest about the Lord's works, James." The padre chided.

"I don't think that you'll be needing that Luger any longer, padre. As far as I'm concerned, the book is yours."

"Well, I suppose that in the light of this discovery it is superfluous." The pistol disappeared into his cassock.

On a sideboard over against the wall was tray with several decanters and some glasses. I went over to them and asked, "Would you care to join me in a drink, padre?"

"I don't mind if I do, James. Whisky with a splash, if you please."

I poured several fingers into a couple of glasses and added a little water from a pitcher. When I returned to the table, I handed one of the glasses to Donnelly.

"It's too bad, really, padre," I said after taking a sip of whisky. "One man dead, one man shot, another driven mad, and a beautiful woman bound for prison, all over a fake. Seems such a waste."

"I wouldn't be so sure of that, James," the padre responded. He picked up a magnifying glass from the table and examined the first page of the codex intently. He was several minutes at it before he carefully closed the cover of the volume.

"I'm no expert, James, but I have some knowledge of such matters. I will swear that this one page is the genuine article. It certainly looks to be hundreds of years old, and the Latin text is—well—authentically profane."

"I'll have to take your word for that, padre. Do you think that the codex has always been a fraud, an empty book full of promises but no contents?"

"Oh, no, James. The codex is real enough. The records of the Vatican Library are quite explicit on that point. It was intact when the Borgia borrowed it. It's some time since then that it has been dismantled or at least the opening page removed."

He opened the book again and used the magnifying glass to examine the page where it had been bound into the spine. He flipped to the next leaf and examined the same area.

"Look here, James. You can see where the first page was sewn in separately. It was done quite expertly, but I'm certain that the page from the codex was added to this volume at some time much later than the original binding."

"Any idea when, padre?"

"Quite recently, by which I mean within the last hundred years or so."

"And the rest of the codex?"

"I can only think that it's out there—somewhere."

There was a look in the padre's eye as if he wasn't seeing what was around him but somewhere quite distant.

"So what now, padre?" I asked, bringing him back to earth.

"Oh, I'll take the codex, what there is of it, back to the Vatican. Then I imagine eventually I'll be sent to look for the rest of it. The other pages must be out there someplace, Vienna, Budapest, Prague, somewhere else."

"Seems like kind of a fool's errand, padre. It's pretty clear to me that the man who sold the codex to Brockington was running a con. There's no reason to think that he has the other pages or knows what became of them."

"No, but it's someplace to start, James," Donnelly said wistfully. He took a sip of his drink and then asked, "Would you care to join me, James? It would be a grand adventure."

"What, go searching for a book that probably doesn't exist?"

"Why not? You could be a big help to me. Wouldn't it be better than seeking out murders and thieves and the like?"

"I'm not even Catholic, padre."

"I'm sure that my superiors would make allowances for someone of your talents, James."

"Thanks for the offer, padre, but I think I'll have to take a pass. I'm happy right where I am here in San Francisco."

"I thought that was what you'd say, James," the padre said with regret.

He began the task of rewrapping the codex in the brown paper it had arrived in. He had some trouble with the string that I had cut, but with a few deft motions he managed to knot the twine.

"I'd appreciate it, James, if you'd refrain from mentioning this, or my presence here—at least until I've had a chance to make good my escape."

"I won't say anything, padre. I don't think Lt. Miller will care. He's got his murderer."

"Well, then I best be off, James. But, before I go, one last toast?"

"I'll drink to that, padre."

"Then, to the Rathcael Codex," he said raising his glass a dashing off the rest of his whisky.

"To the Rathcael Codex," I echoed.

The padre picked up the parcel and tucking it under his arm prepared to leave.

"Aren't you forgetting something, padre?"

"What's that, James?"

"You still have my automatic in your pocket," I reminded him.

"So I do, James. So I do." He reached into his cassock, produced the pistol and placed it on the table.

I picked it up and stuck it back in my holster. When I looked up, the padre had vanished.

CHAPTER 32

If anyone cared that the padre had walked away with the codex, they never said anything to me about it. Brockington was certainly past caring. He was taken to a sanitarium and as far as I know he's still there. Seeing as the codex had disappeared again, I didn't get the five thousand, though I did manage to talk Brockington's lawyers into paying me my expenses.

Miss Lanier's trial proved to be quite a sensation. As a witness, I didn't get a chance to see most of it, but I read all the press accounts. It ran for a week. For a while, it looked as if the jury might actually believe her story, but in the end she got twenty years. I think it was the way that she had shot Fenchurch that convinced the jury that she was guilty.

Fenchurch recovered from his gunshot wound, but I understand his health has suffered in prison. He was tried as an accessory and got eight years.

There were rumors that Conklin had jumped ship in Ecuador and ended up in Australia, but I never followed up on them. The Hungarian went back to Hungary a few days after the case broke. As for the American, he left for his home out East where he still has his millions, which is why I haven't mentioned his name. There's no point in getting sued. The police had never really had anything on either one of them except for the fact that they'd met with Fenchurch, and with the Hungarian being a diplomat and the American being rich, they wisely decided to leave well enough alone.

Miller got a commendation but not much else. I think he's happy with that. I bought him a beer when the trial ended and he seemed content.

I haven't seen the padre since, but I did get a post card from him from Bucharest. There was a picture of some onion domed cathedral on the front. On the back he had written, "Having a miserable time. Wish you were here. Cheers, Father Donnelly."

I kept my promise to Shorty Smith, and over a fifth of rye I gave him all the details of the case as I knew them. His story ran all through the week of the trial. His editor must have been happy with the story, because the next time I ran into Shorty he bought me a drink, which coming from a newspaper man tells you something.

If I told you I never think back over that night on the dance floor with Gail and what might have been, I'd be a liar. I know it was an illusion, and that it never would have worked out, but I still occasionally find myself back in that moment of time. Then I snap out of it and face reality.

SPECIAL PREVIEW!

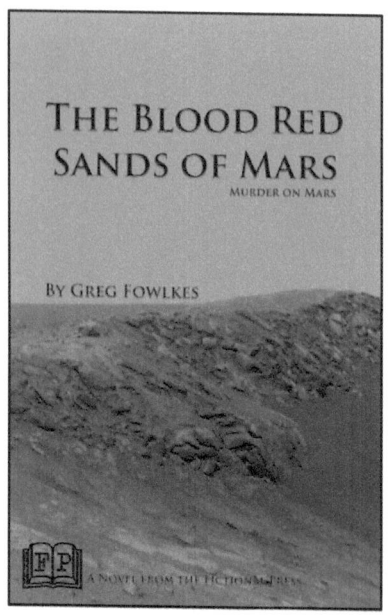

THE BLOOD RED SANDS OF MARS

By Greg Fowlkes

Book One from the Murder on Mars Series

Now available from The Fictional Press
www.TheFictionalPress.com

THE BLOOD RED
SANDS OF MARS

The wind was blowing again against the west wall of the hut. He could hear the grains of sand abrading the thin aluminum skin that protected him from the outside. Through the window, half frosted from the continuous onslaught of sand and dust, he could see clouds of dust obscuring the sky. The sky was a pastel pink, a color no sky had any right to be. The wind, despite its 120 kph. velocity, made only a thin howl as it blew over the half buried cylinder of the hut.

McKernan lay on his cot trying not to admit that he was awake. It was a losing battle. After a few minutes he surrendered and glanced over at the clock sitting on the crate next to his bed. The dim red digits of the LED display read 7:58. It was too early to get up, too late to go back to sleep. He rolled over, shivering at the cold. The temperature couldn't have been more than ten degrees Celsius inside the hut. For the twentieth time he thought to himself that he would have to fix the heater before winter—if he could get the parts. Either that, or put in more insulation—if he could find that. The cold finally forced the decision to get up.

Standing, he felt the cold plastic floor beneath his bare feet. With his foot he fished the worn and patched pants from beneath the cot and pulled them on. He dug underneath his pillow and came up with a switchblade knife that he stuck in his pocket before drawing on the turtleneck sweater that had lain next to his pants. The cold feel of the cloth did nothing to dispel the cold from his body. From the crate he picked up a shoulder holster with a small automatic pistol and put it on. McKernan drew the weapon, worked the slide once, and after examining it perfunctorily, placed it back in the holster. Satisfied, he pulled on a worn pair of leather boots and placed another knife in a sheath between his skin and the boot top.

Dressed, he went over to the shelf that served as counter and table. He put a pan of beans onto the heating unit and got a soysteak from the small refrigerator that held up one end of the shelf. The steak went into the frying pan on the other heating element. An egg would have been nice, but at the current price of three dollars apiece it was an extravagance that he would have to put off for a while.

As the food cooked he drew a liter of water from the spigot in the corner of the hut and watered the plants in the garden under the window. The carrots and tomatoes were doing nicely. He smiled briefly because it would be good to have fresh vegetables for a change. The big, leafy oxygen plants were doing well, too. He would be able to cut down on his oxygen ration this month and save some money.

He took the beans off the heating element and replaced them with the coffee pot. The beans were still half cold, but he wasn't in the mood to hassle with them. He only had the two heating elements, and he didn't want to have to wait for his coffee. He forced down the beans and then wolfed down the steak. It almost tasted like real beef, but then maybe his memories were fading. As usual, the coffee tasted terrible and tepid, too. The air pressure in the hut was too low for water to boil properly.

He finished his meal and scraped the remnants of food into the pressure vessel that served as a compost heap. The gauge on its neighbor showed that he had almost half a tank of methane. He'd be able to sell that soon and use the money for something useful, like a still. Completing his rounds, the gauges on the life support systems showed that everything was still working at keeping him alive. He went back to the pots and scrubbed them clean with sand. That, at least, was plentiful and cheap.

He checked his watch against the clock. It was time to get going. Pulling on his jacket he went to the airlock at the corridor end of the hut. After checking the gauge to make sure that there was pressure on the other side, he undogged the latches and stepped through. Closing the door behind him, he repeated the process with the outer hatch, latching both doors behind him. The outer door he locked with a heavy padlock.

He had entered a low tubular corridor made of the same aluminum foil and plastic foam construction as the hut. The walls, however, were even thinner, and no pretense was made of heating it. He could see his breath condensing in front of him as he began to walk down its length. It was a hell of a way to live, he reflected, not for the first time. But then, it had been hell living in L.A. where he'd been born, with brown air, rats, a chronic shortage of water, and overcrowded tenements. He had made his choice, but sometimes it seemed as though life was a continual shiver.

The corridor was pierced at regular intervals by hatches identical to his own. The huts behind the hatches were identical, too, except for the modifications the owners had made to make them more livable. This part of the city was old, dating back a couple of decades to the first days of the settlement when it had been part of a scientific base. The scientists had departed, at least from that corridor, and been replaced by those who had the money to buy or rent the huts from the Trust Authority. Maintenance was pretty much left up to the residents.

Along the sides and overhead ran the pipes and conduits that pumped in the gases, liquids, and power necessary for sustaining life. The whole system looked as jury rigged and fragile as it actually was, though surprisingly few people died whenever the system failed. Martians were a cautious lot. One didn't talk much about injuries. Accidents on Mars didn't leave many.

A hundred meters down the tube he came to an airlock. Going through the same ritual that he had used on his front door, he went through to another length of corridor indistinguishable from the one he had just left. Continuing on, he passed through two more airlocks until he entered a corridor that sloped downward. The hatches were farther apart, and larger. Signs overhead indicated the businesses or functions that were carried out behind them. The air was warmer because the corridor was buried beneath the sand which provided insulation. At the end of the tunnel was a larger airlock set into a wall of fused silica bricks, the first substantial piece of construction he had met that morning.

Passing through the portal was like entering another world, which in a way he had. This was the public Mars, the planet seen by the corporation men and the officials of the Trust Authority. It was also the planet seen by tourists, the brave new colony, man's first outpost on another planet. The tourists didn't really care to see the hut town. They were part of the same world as the corporation men and the government types. It still took a great deal of money or power to reach Mars.

The difference was more than one of degree. For one thing, the temperature was a comfortable twenty. For another, the walls were flat and met the floors and ceilings at right angles, unlike the inflated skins of the huts and corridors. With a little imagination it could almost be an enclosed shopping mall on earth, though the presence of fused silica blocks was more prevalent than any architect would allow.

The most important difference, however, was the sight of people scurrying along. He hadn't met anyone in the outer corridors. People rarely lingered there because of the cold. Now, McKernan could see at least twenty people and it was still fairly early. No airlocks interrupted this corridor. Extending for two hundred meters in either direction, it was twenty meters wide and ten high, the largest enclosed volume on the planet. Arrayed along its length were the offices and store fronts of the corporations that owned Mars, as well as the more prosperous saloons and bordellos.

One day the Trust Authority promised that the whole city would be like that, with apartments and condominiums for the ordinary workers, but neither the Authority or the corporations had yet come up with the money. For the moment all that existed was the one street of a few blocks.

McKernan headed towards the Authority's offices which dominated one end of the mall, but turned aside at the last moment when he noticed that a small, dark doorway was open. He knew that he should resist the temptation, but he was not in a very disciplined mood. He went through the doorway into the darkness beyond.

Finnegan's was the only real, honest bar on Mars. There were any number of saloons and even a cocktail lounge in the Mars Sheraton, but only one quiet, dark place where a man could drink in peace. McKernan felt the need for some of that peace at the moment.

He sat down on one of the stools before the only mahogany bar on Mars. Finnegan, himself, was behind the bar, though in fact he almost always was, no matter what the hour.   The bartender looked up and greeted the newcomer, "Good morning, constable. Beer or whiskey?"

"It's too early for beer. It's too early for whiskey, but give me a shot, anyway."

Finnegan poured out a shot glass of amber liquid and placed it before McKernan and then stood back polishing a glass while he studied the man opposite him.

McKernan knocked back half the glass before he spoke. When he did, there was a bitter edge to his voice. "Sometimes I wonder if it's worth it, Finnegan. I could be back on a planet fit for human life."

"Could you, now, constable?" Finnegan said, putting down the glass and picking up another in equally gleaming condition. "If mother earth was such a bed of roses, why are you here?"

He breathed on the glass and examined it against the light for a moment, then looked at McKernan with the same intentness. "You're here because you're not the sort to live off the dole or to spend your life with another man being your boss. Instead you'll spend your life trying to make this planet a fit place to live and retire in twenty years with a nice pension. Now drink up and get to work, laddy."

"Yeah, sure. Sorry to burden you with my problems. Early morning depression, I guess. See you." He finished off the shot and left five dollars in Authority script on the bar.

The bite of the whiskey so early in the morning didn't really help his disposition, but it did give him enough courage to make it to the office. The morning ritual at Finnegan's was becoming too much of a habit. His three years on Mars were beginning to show.

The jail wasn't in the brick part of the Authority building, but in the complex of pneumatic architecture that sprawled behind it. The huts were old—older than his own—but dated back to the days when governments had not begrudged a few billions for exploration, back before space had to show a profit. For that reason, they were sound and well insulated, though a bit tacky looking.

The jail consisted of two huts joined together, one for offices, the other for the two makeshift cells and storage. Ferris was the only one there when he walked in, a young kid, younger than he had been himself when he had come to Mars. He was still impressed enough with his responsibilities and had not yet been worn down by the grim realities to take his job in any way but seriously.

Ferris greeted him with a solemn, "Good morning, sir," with a stress on the sir. As a three year veteran of Mars, Ferris looked on his boss with more than a touch of awe.

"Anything exciting happen overnight?" McKernan didn't really expect much. A few fights in the saloon district, a knifing maybe if things got out of hand. Petty thievery, or perhaps not so petty. He looked at Ferris and saw a flash of excitement in his eyes that the younger man was trying hard to suppress in order to match the hard bitten image he had of his superior.

"Yes, sir. We've got a murder on our hands."

"Another knifing down at Thelma's?" he asked, naming an infamous saloon and bordello that figured in a quarter of all the police reports.

"No. A prospector was found out on his claim yesterday, over on the far side of Olympus Mons. He was shot, Inspector."

That was bad, McKernan thought. People on Mars weren't supposed to have guns. With the thin skins of most buildings and a hostile atmosphere outside that would support life exactly as long as you could hold your breath, they were dangerous, and not just to the targets. The Authority had made them illegal and the corporations had been more than willing to agree. They weren't easy to get—not something that could be picked up casually or made, like a knife. Even without the details it sounded like the work of a real criminal and not just a squabble over a claim or a woman.

"Okay. Let me have the report. I'll take a look at it."

He took the folder from Ferris who looked a bit crestfallen. *He probably expects me to go rush off to the outside and track down the murderer like an Indian scout,* McKernan thought. *He'd learn in time.* Mars was a big planet and a dangerous one, but because of its nature there were also very few places that a man could run to and none where he could hide indefinitely.

He was leafing through the report when he came to his door. For the thousandth time he read, "Inspector Erik McKernan, Chief Constable." *Mother would have been proud,* he thought sardonically. She had hated the L.A. cops like all the other residents of the barrio. He went through the door into the little cubicle that was his real home. There, sitting at his desk, he began to read the report, sketchy though it was, to look for some explanations.

The Blood Red Sands of Mars c is available now from The Fictional Press. Find it on TheFictionalPress.com, or buy it on Amazon.com!

THE FICTIONAL DETECTIVE
BY GREG FOWLKES

WHO KILLED EZEKIAL O. HANDLER?

A beautiful dame, a hard-boiled private eye --- and a dead body.

It started like any other case. When a famous writer dies in a mysterious car crash, private detective Frank Slade is called in to find answers, but all he finds is more questions. Who killed Ezekial Handler? Who is Janet Nielsen and why is she so interested in finding out? Who is leaving the neatly typed clues? And as Slade tries to find answers to these questions he starts to wonder if the ultimate answer will threaten his very existence.

Now available from The Fictional Press.
Buy it on Amazon.com!

The Laws of Magic
By Greg Fowlkes

Egil Njalson was an aspiring lawyer. A lawyer with a difference. Not only had he passed the bar, but he had an undergraduate degree from the most prestigious school of magic in the country, the California Institute of Thaumaturgy. Needless to say his caseload and clients tended to the unusual. Like witches; or vampires. And the opposition, well they were likely to be demons. But Egil Njalson had sworn an oath to uphold the law of the land, and...

The Laws of Magic

Now available from The Fictional Press.
Buy it on Amazon.com!

The Fictional Press
www.TheFictionalPress.com

About The Fictional Press

The Fictional Press, an imprint of Intrepid Ink, LLC, provides full publishing services to authors of fiction and non-fiction books, eBooks and websites. From editing to formatting, to publishing, to marketing, Intrepid Ink gets your creative works into the hands of the people who want to read them.

Find out more at www.thefictionalpress.com.

www.ingramcontent.com/pod-product-compliance
Lightning Source LLC
Chambersburg PA
CBHW020054030726
47498CB00006B/1777